Killing Eve: Codename Villanelle

Luke Jennings

JOHN MURRAY

First published in 2017 by John Murray (Publishers)
An Hachette UK Company

First published in paperback in 2018

15

A CIP catalogue record for this title is available from the British Library

UK Paperback ISBN 978-1-473-66641-2
Export Paperback ISBN 978-1-473-69942-7
Ebook ISBN 978-1-473-66640-5

Typeset in Sabon MT by Hewer Text UK Ltd, Edinburgh
Printed and bound by Clays Ltd, Elcograf S.p.A.

John Murray policy is to use papers that are natural, renewable
and recyclable products and made from wood grown in sustainable
forests. The logging and manufacturing processes are expected to
conform to the environmental regulations of the country of origin.

John Murray (Publishers)
Carmelite House
50 Victoria Embankment
London EC4Y 0DZ

www.johnmurray.co.uk

APR
24

I

The Palazzo Falconieri stands on a promontory on one of the smaller Italian lakes. It's late June, and a faint breeze touches the pines and cypresses that cluster like sentinels around the rocky headland. The gardens are imposing, and perhaps even beautiful, but the deep shadows lend the place a forbidding air, which is echoed by the severe lines of the Palazzo itself.

The building faces the lake, and is fronted by tall windows through which silk curtains are visible. The east wing was once a banqueting hall, but now functions as a conference room. At its centre, beneath a heavy art deco chandelier, is a long table bearing a Bugatti bronze of a panther.

At first glance the twelve men sitting around the table look ordinary enough. Successful, judging from their quietly expensive clothes. Most are in their late fifties or early sixties, with the kind of faces that you instantly forget. There is an unblinking watchfulness about these men, however, which is not ordinary.

The morning passes in discussion, which is conducted in Russian and English, the languages common to all those present. Then a light lunch — antipasti, lake trout, chilled Vernaccia wine, fresh figs and apricots — is served on the terrace. Afterwards the twelve men pour themselves coffee, contemplate the breeze-ruffled expanse of the lake, and pace the garden. There are no security people, because at this level of secrecy, security people themselves become a risk. Before long the men have returned to their places in the shadowed conference room. The day's agenda is simply headed 'EUROPE'.

The first speaker is an ageless, darkly tanned figure with deep-set eyes. He looks around him. 'This morning, gentlemen, we discussed Europe's political and economic future. We talked, in particular, about the flow of capital, and how this can best be controlled. This afternoon I want to speak to you about a different economy.' The room darkens, and the twelve turn to face the screen on the room's north wall showing an image of a Mediterranean port, of container ships and ship-to-shore gantry cranes.

'Palermo, gentlemen, today the principal point of entry for cocaine into Europe. The result of a strategic alliance between the Mexican drug cartels and the Sicilian Mafia.'

'Aren't the Sicilians a spent force?' asks a heavyset man to his left. 'I was under the impression that the mainland syndicates ran the drugs trade these days.'

'That used to be the case. Until eighteen months ago the cartels dealt principally with the 'Ndrangheta, from the southern Italian region of Calabria. But in recent months a war has broken out between the Calabrians, and a resurgent Sicilian clan, the Greci.'

A face appears on the screen. The dark eyes coldly watchful. The mouth a steel trap.

'Salvatore Greco has dedicated his life to resurrecting the influence of his family, which lost its place in the Cosa Nostra power structure in the 1990s, following the murder of Salvatore's father by a member of the rival Matteo family. A quarter of a century later Salvatore has hunted down and killed all of the surviving Mattei. The Greci, and their associates the Messini, are the richest, most powerful, and most feared of the Sicilian clans. Salvatore is known to have personally murdered at least sixty people, and to have ordered the deaths of hundreds more. Today, at fifty-five years of age, his hold over Palermo and its drug trade is absolute. His enterprises, worldwide, turn over some twenty to thirty billion dollars. Gentlemen, he's practically one of us.'

A faint ripple of amusement, or something approximating to it, runs around the room.

'The problem with Salvatore Greco is not his predilection for torture and murder,' he continues. 'When mafiosi kill mafiosi it's like a self-cleaning oven. But recently he has started ordering the assassination of members of the establishment. To date, his tally is two judges and four senior magistrates, all killed by car bombs, and an investigative journalist, who was gunned down last month outside her apartment. The journalist was pregnant at the time of her death. The child did not survive.'

He pauses, and raises his glance to the screen with the image of the dead woman, spreadeagled on the pavement in a pool of blood.

'Needless to say, it has not been possible to directly implicate Greco in any of these crimes. Police have been bribed or threatened, witnesses intimidated. The code of silence, or *omertà*, prevails. The man is, to all intents and purposes, untouchable. A month ago I sent an intermediary to arrange a meeting with him, as I felt that we needed to reach some sort of accommodation. His activities in this corner of

3

Europe have become so excessive that they threaten to impact on our own interests. Greco's response was immediate. The following day I received a sealed package.' The image on the screen changes. 'It contained, as you can see, my associate's eyes, ears and tongue. The message was clear. No meeting. No discussion. No accommodation.'

The men around the table regard the grisly tableau for a moment, then return their gaze to the speaker.

'Gentlemen, I think we need to take an executive decision concerning Salvatore Greco. He is a dangerously uncontrollable force, and beyond the reach of the law. His criminal activities, and the social havoc they entail, threaten the stability of the Mediterranean sector. I propose that we remove him from the game, permanently.'

Rising from his chair, the speaker makes his way to a side-table, returning with an antique lacquered box. Taking out a black velvet drawstring bag, he pours its contents on the table in front of him. Twenty-four small ivory fish, twelve of them aged to a smooth yellow, twelve of them stained a dark blood-red. Each man receives a contrasting pair of fish.

The velvet bag makes its way around the table counter-clockwise. When it has made a full revolution, it is passed to the man who proposed the vote. Once again, the contents of the bag are poured onto the dimly gleaming surface of the table. Twelve red fish. A unanimous sentence of death.

It's evening, a fortnight later, and Villanelle is sitting at an outside table at Le Jasmin, a private members club in Paris's Sixteenth Arrondissement. From the east comes the murmur of traffic on the Boulevard Suchet, to the west is the Bois de Boulogne and the Auteuil racecourse. The club's garden is bordered by a trellis hung with blossoming jasmine whose scent infuses the warm air. Most of the other tables are occupied, but conversation is muted. The light fades, the night awaits.

Villanelle takes a long sip of her Grey Goose vodka Martini, and discreetly surveys the surroundings, particularly noting the couple at the next table. Both are in their mid-twenties: he elegantly dishevelled, she cat-like and exquisite. Are they brother and sister? Professional colleagues? Lovers?

Definitely not brother and sister, Villanelle decides. There's a tension between them – a complicity – that's anything but familial. They're certainly rich, though. Her silk sweater, for example, its dark gold matching her eyes. Not new, but definitely Chanel. And they're drinking vintage Taittinger, which doesn't come cheap at Le Jasmin.

Catching Villanelle's eye, the man raises his champagne flute a centimetre or two. He murmurs to his companion, who fixes her with a cool, assessing stare.

'Would you like to join us?' she asks. It's a challenge, as much as an invitation.

Villanelle stares back, unblinking. A breeze shivers the scented air.

'It's not compulsory,' says the man, his wry smile at odds with the calm of his gaze.

Villanelle stands, lifts her glass. 'I'd love to join you. I was expecting a friend, but she must have been held up.'

'In that case . . .' The man rises to his feet. 'I'm Olivier. And this is Nica.'

'Villanelle.'

The conversation unfolds conventionally enough. Olivier, she learns, has recently launched a career as an art dealer. Nica intermittently works as an actress. They are not related, nor on closer inspection do they give the impression of being lovers. Even so, there is something subtly erotic in their complicity, and the way they've drawn her into their orbit.

'I'm a day-trader,' Villanelle tells them. 'Currencies, interest-rate futures, all that.' With satisfaction, she notes the immediate dimming of interest in their eyes. She can, if necessary, talk for hours about day-trading, but they don't want to know. Instead, Villanelle describes the sunlit first-floor flat in Versailles from which she works. It doesn't exist, but she can picture it down to the ironwork scrolls on the balcony and the faded Persian rug on the floor. Her cover story is perfect now, and deception, as always, affords her a rush of pleasure.

'We love your name, and your eyes, and your hair, and most of all we love your shoes,' says Nica.

Villanelle laughs, and flexes her feet in her strappy satin Louboutins. Catching Olivier's eye, she deliberately mirrors his languid posture. She imagines his hands moving knowledgeably and possessively over her. He would see her, she guesses, as a beautiful, collectible object. He would think himself in control.

'What's funny?' asks Nica, tilting her head and lighting a cigarette.

'You are,' says Villanelle. How would it be, she wonders, to lose herself in that golden gaze? To feel that smoky mouth on hers. She's enjoying herself now; she knows that both Olivier and Nica want her. They think that they're playing her, and Villanelle will go on letting them think so. It will be amusing to manipulate them, to see how far they will go.

6

'I have a suggestion,' says Olivier, and at that moment the phone in Villanelle's bag begins to blink. A one-word text: DEFLECT. She stands, her expression blank. She glances at Nica and Olivier, but in her mind they no longer exist. She's out of there without a word, and in less than a minute is swinging into a northbound stream of traffic on her Vespa.

It's three years now since she first met the man who sent her the text. The man who, to this day, she knows only as Konstantin. Her circumstances, then, were very different. Her name was Oxana Vorontsova, and she was officially registered as a student of French and Linguistics at the University of Perm, in central Russia. In six months' time she was due to sit her finals. It was unlikely, however, that she would ever walk into the university's examination hall as, since the previous autumn, she'd been unavoidably detained elsewhere. Specifically, in the Dobryanka women's remand centre in the Ural Mountains. Accused of murder.

It's a short drive, perhaps five minutes, from Le Jasmin to Villanelle's apartment near the Porte de Passy. The 1930s building is large, anonymous and quiet, with a well-secured underground garage. After parking the Vespa alongside her car, a fast and anonymous silver-grey Audi TT Roadster, Villanelle takes the lift to the sixth floor, and ascends the short flight of stairs to her rooftop apartment. The front door, although faced with the same panelling as the others in the building, is of reinforced steel, and the electronic locking system is custom-made.

Inside, the apartment is comfortable and spacious, even a little shabby. Konstantin handed Villanelle the keys and title deeds a year ago. She has no idea who lived there before her, but the place was fully furnished when she moved in, and from the decades-old fixtures and fittings, she guesses it was someone elderly. Uninterested in decoration, she has left the apartment as she found it, with its faded sea-green and French-blue rooms, and its nondescript post-Impressionist paintings.

No one ever visits her here – her professional meetings take place in cafes and public parks, her sexual liaisons are mostly conducted in hotels – but if they were to do so, the apartment would bear out her cover story in every detail. In the study, her computer, a top-of-the-range wafer of stainless steel, is protected by civilian security software that a halfway skilled hacker would quickly bypass. But a scan of its contents would reveal little more than the details of a successful day-trading account, and the contents of the filing cabinet are similarly non-committal. There is no music system. Music, for Villanelle, is at best a pointless irritation and at worst a lethal danger. In silence lies safety.

Conditions at the remand centre were unspeakable. The food was barely edible, the sanitation non-existent, and an icy, numbing wind from the Dobryanka river penetrated every cheerless corner of the institution. The slightest infraction of the rules resulted in a prolonged period of *shiza*, or solitary confinement. Oxana had been there for three months when she was ordered from her cell, marched without explanation to the prison courtyard, and ordered to climb into a battered all-terrain vehicle. Two hours later, deep in the Perm Krai, the driver halted by a bridge over the frozen Chusovaya river, and wordlessly directed her to a low, prefabricated unit, beside which a black four-wheel-

at the orphanage, during which time the staff noted your exceptional academic skills. They also identified other traits, including habitual bed-wetting and a near-total inability to form relationships with other children.'

She exhaled, the smoke a long grey plume in the cold air, and touched the tip of her tongue to a ridge of scar tissue on her upper lip. The gesture, like the scar itself, was barely perceptible, but the man in the coat saw it, and noted it.

'When you were ten your father was seconded again, this time to Dagestan. You returned to the Sakharov orphanage where, after three months, you were discovered setting fire to the dormitory block, and transferred to the psychiatric unit of Municipal Hospital Number 4 in Perm. Against the advice of your therapist, who had diagnosed you as suffering from a sociopathic personality disorder, you were returned home to your father. The following year you commenced your studies at Industrialny District secondary school. Here, once again, you won praise for your academic results – particularly for your language skills – and once again it was noted that you made no attempt to make friends or form relationships. Indeed, it's on the record that you were involved in, and suspected of instigating, a number of violent incidents.

'You did, however, form an attachment to your French teacher, a Miss Leonova, and became extremely agitated when you learned that she had been subjected to a serious sexual assault while waiting for a bus late at night. Her supposed assailant was arrested but later released for lack of evidence. Six weeks later he was discovered in woodland near the Mulyanka river, incoherent with shock and blood loss. He had been castrated with a knife. Doctors succeeded in saving his life but his attacker was never identified. At the time of these events you were approaching your seventeenth birthday.'

She trod out her cigarette on the floor. 'Is this leading anywhere?'

He almost smiled. 'I could mention the gold medal you won for pistol shooting at the University Games in Ekaterinburg. In your first year as an undergraduate.'

She shrugged, and he leaned forward in his chair. 'Just between ourselves. Those three men in the Pony Club, what did you feel when you killed them?'

She met his gaze, her expression blank.

'OK, hypothetically. What might you have felt?'

'At the time, I might have felt satisfaction at a job well done. Now . . .' She shrugged again. 'Nothing.'

'So for nothing, you are looking at twenty years in Berezniki, or somewhere similar?'

'You brought me all the way here to tell me that?'

'The truth, Oxana Borisovna, is that the world has a problem with people like you. Men or women who are born, as you were, without a conscience, or the ability to feel guilt. You represent a tiny fraction of the population at large, but without you . . .' He lit another cigarette, and sat back in his chair. 'Without predators, people who can think the unthinkable, and act without fear or hesitation, the world stands still. You are an evolutionary necessity.'

There was a long silence. His words confirmed what she had always known, even at her lowest ebb: that she was different, that she was special, that she was born to soar. She stared through the window at the waiting vehicle, and the guards stamping their feet in the snow. Again, the tip of her tongue momentarily probed her upper lip.

'So what do you want from me?' she asked.

Konstantin told her, sparing no detail of what was to come. And listening to him, it was as if everything in her life had led to that moment. Her expression never flickered, but the thrill that ripped through her was as avid as hunger.

Over Paris, the light is fading. From a drawer in the desk in her study, Villanelle takes a new, boxed Apple laptop, and unpacks it. Soon she is connected to a Gmail account and is opening a message whose subject heading is *Jeff and Sarah – Holiday Pics*. There are two paragraphs of text, and a dozen JPEG images of a couple exploring tourist sites in and around Cairo.

> *Hi All!*
>
> *We've had the best time ever. Pyramids amazing, and Sarah rode a camel (see attached pics)! Back on Sunday, landing 7.42, should be home by 9.45. Best wishes – Jeff.*
>
> *PS please note Sarah's new email SMPrice88307@ gmail.com*

Ignoring the letters and words Villanelle extracts the figures. These make up a one-time password, which enables her to access the compressed data embedded in the innocent-looking JPEG images. She remembers the words of the Indian systems designer who taught her covert communication: 'Encrypted messages are all very well, but even if they're completely unbreakable, they attract attention. Much better to ensure that no one suspects the existence of the message in the first place.'

She turns to the photographs. Because they're highly detailed, with excellent resolution, they can carry a substantial data payload. Ten minutes later she has extracted all of the concealed text, which she combines into a single document.

A second email headed *Steve's mobile* has a briefer message, just a single phone number, and six JPEG images of an amateur football game. Villanelle repeats the earlier process, but this time extracts a series of photographic portraits. They are all of the same man. His eyes are dark, almost black, and the set of his mouth is hard. Villanelle stares at the pictures. She has never seen the man before, but there's something in his face that she recognises. A kind of emptiness. It takes her a moment to remember where she's seen that look before. In the mirror. In her own eyes. The text document is headed *Salvatore Greco*.

One of the unique attributes that recommended Villanelle to her present employers was her photographic memory. It takes her thirty minutes to read the Greco file, and when she has finished she can recall every page as if she were holding it in front of her. Culled from police files, surveillance logs, court records, and informers' statements, it is an exhaustive personal portrait. All things considered, though, it is frustratingly brief. A timeline of Greco's career to date. An FBI psychological profile. A breakdown, in large part hypothetical, of his domestic situation, personal habits and sexual proclivities. A list of properties held in his name. An analysis of his known security arrangements.

The portrait that emerges is of a man of austere tastes. Pathologically averse to public attention, he is extremely skilled at avoiding it, even in an era of mass communication. At the same time his power stems in large part from his reputation. In a region of the world where torture and murder are routine, Greco's ferocity sets him apart. Anyone who dares to stand in his way or question his authority is eliminated, usually with spectacular cruelty. Rivals have seen their entire families shot, informers discovered with their throats slashed and their tongues drawn out through the gaping wounds.

Villanelle looks out over the city. To the left, the Eiffel Tower is silhouetted against the evening sky. To the right is the dark mass of the Tour Montparnasse. She considers Greco. Sets his personal refinement against the baroque horror of his actions and commissions. Is there any way she can turn this contradiction to her advantage?

She re-reads the document file, scanning each sentence for a possible entrée. Greco's principal residence, a farmhouse in a hill-village outside Palermo, is a fortress. His family lives there, protected by a loyal and vigilant team of armed bodyguards. His wife, Calogera, rarely leaves home; his only daughter, Valentina, lives in a neighbouring village, where she is married to the oldest son of her father's *consigliere*. The region has its own dialect and a history of obdurate hostility to outsiders. Those whom Greco wishes to meet – allied clan members, prospective associates, his tailor, his barber – are invited to the farmhouse, where they are searched, and if necessary disarmed. When Greco leaves home to visit his mistress in Palermo, he is invariably accompanied by an armed driver and at least two bodyguards. There appears to be no predictable pattern to these visits.

One document in particular, though, interests Villanelle. It's a five-year-old press cutting from the Italian newspaper *Corriere della Sera* reporting a near-fatal accident sustained by one of the paper's own journalists in Rome. According

15

to Bruno De Santis: 'I was coming out of a restaurant in Trastevere when a car came racing towards me on the wrong side of the street. The next thing I knew, I was in hospital, lucky to be alive.'

De Santis's none-too-subtle suggestion is that this attempt on his life is the consequence of a piece he wrote for the *Corriere* a month earlier, about a young Sicilian soprano named Franca Farfaglia. In the piece, he criticised Farfaglia for having accepted a donation towards her studies at the La Scala Theatre Academy in Milan from Salvatore Greco, 'the notorious organised crime boss'.

It is a brave and perhaps foolhardy piece of journalism, but Villanelle is not interested in De Santis. Instead, she wonders what inspired Greco's generosity towards Farfaglia – not that he couldn't afford an infinity of such gestures. Was it a love of opera, the wish to help a talented local girl to achieve her potential, or an altogether more basic desire?

An Internet search produces a wealth of images of Farfaglia. Commanding in appearance, with proud, severe features, she looks older than her twenty-six years. Several of the images reappear on the singer's own website, where there's a history of her career to date, a selection of performance reviews, and her schedule for the next few months. Scrolling through the engagements, Villanelle pauses. Her eyes narrow, and she touches a fingertip to the scar on her lip. Then, clicking on the hyperlink, she brings up the website of the Teatro Massimo in Palermo.

Oxana's training took the best part of a year.

The worst came first. Six weeks of fitness training and unarmed combat on a lonely, wind-scoured stretch of the

Essex coast. She arrived in early December. The instructor was a former Special Boat Service instructor named Frank, a knotty, taciturn figure of about sixty, with a gaze as cold as the North Sea. His habitual get-up, worn in all weathers, was a faded cotton tracksuit and a pair of old tennis shoes. Frank was merciless. Oxana was underweight and in poor condition following her months in the Dobryanka remand centre, and for the first fortnight the interminable runs across the marshes, with the sleet whipping at her face and the greasy coastal mud sucking at her boots, were torture.

Determination kept her going. Anything, even death from exposure on the mudflats, was better than returning to the Russian penal system. Frank didn't know who she was, and didn't care. His brief was simply to bring her to combat readiness. For the duration of the course she lived in an unheated Nissen hut on a mud-and-shingle island linked to the mainland by a quarter-mile-long causeway. During the Cold War, the place had been an early warning station, and something of its grim, apocalyptic purpose lingered.

On the first night Oxana was so cold she couldn't sleep, but from then on exhaustion took its toll, and she was wrapped in her single blanket and dead to the world by 9 p.m. Frank kicked the corrugated-iron door open every morning at 4 a.m. before tossing her the day's rations – usually a plastic canteen of water and a couple of tins of processed meat and vegetables – and leaving her to pull on her T-shirt, combat trousers and boots, invariably still sodden from the day before. For two hours they ran repeated circuits of the island, either across the oozing grey mudflats or along the icy tideline, before returning to the Nissen hut to brew tea and heat up a mess-tin of rations on a small hexamine stove. By sunrise,

17

they would be outside again, pounding the mudflats until Oxana was vomiting with fatigue.

In the afternoons, as the darkness closed in, they worked on hand-to-hand combat. Over the years Frank had taken elements of ju-jitsu, street-fighting and other techniques and refined them into a single discipline. The emphasis was on improvisation and speed, and practice sessions were often conducted knee-deep in the sea, with the mud and shingle shifting treacherously beneath their feet. Realising that her English was poor, Frank taught by physical example. Oxana thought she knew a thing or two about fighting, having learnt the basics of the Systema Spetsnaz from her father, but Frank seemed to anticipate every move she attempted, deflecting her blows with casual ease before pitching her, yet again, into the icy seawater.

Oxana didn't think she'd ever hated anyone as much as she hated the ex-SBS instructor. No one, even in the Perm orphanage or the Dobryanka remand unit, had so systematically belittled and humiliated her. Hatred became a simmering rage. She was Oxana Borisovna Vorontsova, and she lived by rules that few would even begin to understand. She would beat this *angliski ublyodok*, this donkey-fucker, if it killed her.

Late one afternoon in the final week they were circling each other in the incoming tide. Frank had a Gerber knife with an eight-inch blade, Oxana was unarmed. Frank moved first, swinging the oxidised blade so close to her face that she felt the breeze of its passing, and in response she ducked under his knife-arm and hammered a short-arm punch into his ribs. It stopped him for a second, and by the time the Gerber came slicing back she was out of reach. They danced back and forth, and Frank lunged for her chest. Her body outraced her brain. Half-turning she grabbed his wrist, wrenched him in the direction to which he was already committed, and booted his legs from under him. As Frank fell backwards into the water, arms flailing, she was already lifting her knee to stamp his knife-hand into the shingle – 'Control the weapon, then the man' her father had always told her – and as the instructor involuntarily released the Gerber, fell forwards to pin him underwater. Straddling him, she forced his head back with the palm of her hand, and watched the agonised working of his face as he began to drown.

It was interesting – fascinating, even – but she wanted him alive to acknowledge her triumph, so she dragged him onto the shore, where he rolled onto his side and retched up gouts of seawater. When he finally opened his eyes, she was holding the point of the Gerber knife to his throat. Meeting her eyes, he nodded in submission.

A week later, Konstantin came to collect her, looking her up and down with quiet approval as she waited, rucksack slung loosely over one shoulder, on the muddy track leading to the causeway. 'You look good,' he said, his flat gaze taking in her newly confident stance and windburned, salt-blistered features.

'You know she's a fucking psycho,' said Frank.

'Nobody's perfect,' said Konstantin.

Two days later Oxana flew to Germany for three weeks' escape and evasion training at the mountain warfare school in Mittenwald. She was attached to a NATO Special Forces cadre, and her cover story was that she was on secondment from a Russian Interior Ministry counter-terrorism unit. On the second night, while dug into deep snow, she felt stealthy fingers at the zip of her bivvy bag. A silent but furious fight erupted in the darkness, and the following day two of the NATO soldiers were helicoptered off the mountain, one with a severed forearm tendon, the other with a stab wound through the palm of his hand. After that, no one bothered her.

Immediately after Mittenwald, she was flown to a US Army facility in Fort Bragg, North Carolina, where she was put through an advanced Resistance to Interrogation programme. This was calculatedly nightmarish, and designed to induce maximal stress and anxiety in its subjects. Shortly after her arrival Oxana was stripped naked by her male guards and marched to a brightly lit, windowless cell, empty except for a close-circuit camera mounted high on one wall. Time passed, hour after endless hour, but she was given only water, and without toilet facilities was forced to use the floor. Before long the cell stank, and her stomach was twisting with hunger. If she tried to sleep, the cell would reverberate with white noise, or with electronic voices repeating meaningless phrases at ear-splitting volume.

At the end of the second day – or it might have been the third – she was hooded, and led to another part of the building where she was questioned, in fluent Russian and for hours on end, by unseen interrogators. Between these sessions, in which she was offered food in exchange for information, she was forced to adopt agonising and humiliating stress positions. Starved, sleep-deprived and severely disoriented, she drifted into a trance-like state, in which the boundaries between her senses blurred. She managed, nevertheless, to hang on to some vestigial sense of self, and to the knowledge that the experience would come to an end. However terrifying and degrading it turned out to be, it was preferable to life in the secure wing of a Ural Mountains penal colony. By the time the exercise was officially pronounced over, Oxana was beginning, in a deeply perverse way, to enjoy it.

Further courses followed. A month of weapons familiarisation at a camp to the south of Kiev, in Ukraine, followed by three more at a Russian sniper school. This was not the high-profile establishment outside Moscow where the Spetsnaz Alfa and Vympel detachments trained, but a much more remote facility near Ekaterinburg, run by a private security company whose instructors asked no questions. Being back in Russia felt strange to Oxana, even under the false identity provided by Konstantin. Ekaterinburg, after all, was less than two hundred miles from where she had grown up.

It wasn't long, though, before the deception began to give her a certain heady satisfaction. 'Officially, Oxana Vorontsova no longer exists,' Konstantin informed her. 'A certificate issued at Perm Regional Clinical Hospital indicates that she hanged herself in her cell at the Dobryanka remand centre. District records show that she was buried at public expense in the Industrialny cemetery. Trust me, no one misses her, and no one is looking for her.'

Severka urban sniper school was built around a deserted town. In Soviet times it had been home to a thriving community of scientists studying the effects of radiation exposure; now it was a ghost town, peopled only by life-sized target dummies, strategically situated behind plate-glass windows and at the wheels of rusting, skeletal vehicles. It was an eerie place, silent except for the wind that whistled between its empty buildings.

Oxana's basic training was with the standard-issue Dragunov. Soon, though, she graduated to the VSS, or Special Sniper Rifle. With its exceptionally light weight and integral silencer, it was the ideal urban weapon. By the time she left Severka she had fired thousands of rounds under a variety of operational conditions, and in less than a minute was able to arrive at a firing point with the VSS in its polystyrene case, assemble the weapon, zero the sights, calculate windspeed and other vectors, and squeeze off a lethal head or body-shot ('one shot, one kill', in the words of her instructor) at a range of up to four hundred metres.

Oxana sensed herself changing, and the results pleased her. Her observational ability, sensory skills and reactive speeds had all been extraordinarily enhanced. Psychologically, she felt invulnerable, but then she had always known that she was different from those around her. She felt none of the things they felt. Where others would experience pain or horror, she knew only a frozen dispassion. She had learned to imitate the emotional responses of others – their fears, their uncertainties, their desperate need for affection – but she had never fully experienced them. She knew, however, that if she was to escape notice in the world it was essential to wear a mask of normality, and to disguise the extent of her difference.

She had learnt, very young, that people could be manipulated. Sex was useful in this regard, and Oxana acquired a voracious appetite. Not so much for the act itself, although this had its satisfactions, as for the thrill of pursuit and psychic domination. For lovers, she liked to choose authority figures. Her conquests had included schoolteachers of both genders, a Spetsnaz colleague of her father's, a young woman from a military academy in Kazan against whom she was competing in the University Games, and most satisfying of all, the psychotherapist she'd been referred to for assessment in her first year at university. Oxana had never felt the slightest need to be liked, but it gave her profound satisfaction to be desired. To see the look in her conquest's eyes – that final melting of resistance – which told her the transfer of power was complete.

Not that it was ever quite enough. Because for all its fierce excitement, that moment of submission invariably marked the end of Oxana's interest. The story was always the same, even with Yuliana, the psychotherapist. By yielding to Oxana, by surrendering her mystery, she made herself undesirable. And Oxana simply moved on, leaving the older woman bereft, her personal and professional self-esteem in tatters.

After the sniper course, she learnt about explosives and toxicology in Volgograd, surveillance in Berlin, advanced driving and lock-picking in London, and identity management, communications and coding in Paris. For Oxana, who had never left Russia before her appointment with Konstantin at the Chusovaya Bridge, the international travelling was dizzying. Each course was taught in the language of the country in question, testing her linguistic aptitude to the limit and, more often than not, leaving her mentally as well as physically drained.

Throughout it all, patient and imperturbable on the sidelines, was Konstantin. He maintained a professional distance between himself and Oxana, but was sympathetic towards her on the handful of occasions when the pressure became too much, and she demanded, coldly, to be left alone. 'Take a day off,' he told her on one occasion in

London. 'Go and explore the city. And start thinking about your cover name. Oxana Vorontsova's dead.'

By November, her training was almost over. She had been staying in a dingy one-star hotel in the Paris suburb of Belleville, and travelling every day to an anonymous office building in La Défense, where a young man of Indian origin was teaching her the finer points of steganography – the science of concealing secret information in computer files. On the final day of the course Konstantin appeared, paid her hotel bill, and accompanied her to an apartment on the Quai Voltaire, on the Left Bank.

The first-floor apartment was furnished with spare, minimal chic. Its occupant was a tiny, fierce-looking woman of about sixty, dressed completely in black, whom Konstantin introduced as Fantine.

Fantine stared at Oxana, appeared unimpressed by what she saw, and asked her to walk around the room. Self-conscious in her faded T-shirt, jeans and trainers, Oxana complied. Fantine watched her for a moment, turned to Konstantin, and shrugged.

And so began the final stage of Oxana's transformation. She moved into a four-star hotel two streets away, and each morning joined Fantine for breakfast in the first-floor apartment. At nine o'clock every morning a car came for them. On the first day they went to the Galeries Lafayette on Boulevard Haussmann. Fantine marched Oxana round the department store, ordering her to try on a succession of outfits – daywear, casual, evening – and buying them whether Oxana liked them or not. The tight, flashy clothes to which Oxana was drawn Fantine dismissed without a glance.

'I'm trying to teach you Parisian style, *chérie*, not how to dress like a Moscow streetwalker, which you obviously know how to do already.'

By the end of the day, the car was piled high with shopping bags, and Oxana was beginning to enjoy the company of her ruthlessly critical mentor. Over the week that followed they visited shoe shops and fashion houses, couture and prêt-à-porter shows, a vintage emporium in St Germain, and the costume and design museum at the Palais Galliera. At each of these, Fantine offered an unsparing commentary. This was chic, clever and elegant; that was crass, tasteless, and irredeemably vulgar. One afternoon Fantine took Oxana to a hairdresser in the Place des Victoires. Her instructions to the stylist were to proceed as she chose, and to ignore anything that Oxana suggested. Afterwards, Fantine stood her in front of a mirror, and Oxana ran a hand through her short, blunt-cut hair. She liked the look that Fantine had put together for her. The designer biker jacket, the stripy T-shirt, the low-rise jeans and ankle boots. She looked . . . Parisian.

Later that afternoon, they visited a boutique selling scent on the rue du Faubourg Saint-Honoré. 'Choose,' said Fantine. 'But choose well.' For ten minutes Oxana stalked the elegant shop floor, before stopping in front of a glass display cabinet. The assistant watched her for a moment. '*Vous permettez, Mademoiselle?*' he murmured, handing her a slender glass phial with a scarlet ribbon at its neck. Cautiously, Oxana touched the amber scent to her wrist. Fresh as a spring dawn, but with darker base notes, it spoke to something deep inside her.

'It's called Villanelle,' said the assistant. 'It was the favourite scent of the Comtesse du Barry. The perfume house added the red ribbon after she was guillotined in 1793.'

'I shall have to be careful, then,' said Oxana.

Two days later, Konstantin came to collect her from the hotel. 'My cover name,' she said. 'I've chosen it.'

As she crosses the Piazza Verdi in Palermo, her heels clicking faintly on the cobblestones, Villanelle glances up at the imposing frontage of Sicily's, and indeed Italy's, largest opera house. Palm trees rise from the piazza, their leaves whispering faintly in the warm breeze; bronze lions flank the broad entrance stairway. Villanelle is wearing a silk Valentino dress and elbow-length Fratelli Orsini opera gloves. The dress is red, but so darkly shaded as to be almost black. A spacious Fendi shoulder bag hangs by a slim chain. Villanelle's face is pale in the evening light, and her hair is pinned up with a long, curved clip. She looks glamorous, if less showy than the socialites in Versace and Dolce & Gabbana thronging the mirrored entrance hall. First nights at the Teatro Massimo are always an occasion, and tonight's offering is Puccini's *Tosca*, one of the most popular operas of all. That the title role is being sung by a local soprano, Franca Farfaglia, makes the occasion unmissable.

Villanelle buys a programme and moves through the entrance hall to the vestibule. The place is filling fast. There's a buzz of conversation, the muted clink of glasses and an aroma of expensive scent. Ornate wall-lights paint the marble decorations with a soft lemon glow. At the bar she orders a mineral water, and notices that she is being watched by a lean, dark-haired figure.

'Can I get you something more . . . interesting?' he asks, as she pays for her drink. 'A glass of champagne perhaps?'

She smiles. He is thirty-five, she guesses, give or take a year or two. Saturnine good looks. His silver-grey shirt is impeccable and his lightweight blazer looks like Brioni. But his Italian has the rasp of Sicily, and there's an edge of threat in his gaze.

'I won't,' she says. 'Thank you.'

'Let me guess. You're obviously not Italian, even though you speak the language. French?'

'Sort of. It's complicated.'

'So do you like Puccini operas?'

'Of course,' she murmurs. 'Although *La Bohème* is my favourite.'

'That's because you're French.' He holds out his hand. 'Leoluca Messina.'

'Sylviane Morel.'

'So what brings you to Palermo, Mademoiselle Morel?'

She is tempted to terminate the conversation. To walk away. But he might follow, which would make things worse. 'I'm staying with friends.'

'Who?'

'No one you'd know, I'm afraid.'

'You'd be surprised who I know. And trust me, everyone here knows me.'

Half turning, Villanelle allows a sudden smile to light her face. She waves towards the entrance. 'Will you excuse me, Signor Messina. My friends are here.' That was less than convincing, she reproves herself as she edges through the crowd. But there's something about Leoluca Messina – some long acquaintanceship with violence – that makes her want him to forget her face.

Will Greco come, Villanelle wonders, moving through the crowd with vague purpose, scanning the faces around her as she goes. According to Konstantin's local contact, who has had several of the front-of-house staff discreetly bribed and questioned, the Mafia boss comes to most of the important first nights. He always arrives at the last moment and takes the same box, which he occupies alone, with bodyguards stationed outside. Whether he has actually booked to come tonight has, frustratingly, been impossible to establish. But his protégée Farfaglia is singing the lead soprano role. The odds are good.

At considerable cost, Konstantin's people have secured the neighbouring box to the one Greco favours. It is on the first tier, almost directly adjacent to the stage. With ten minutes to curtain-up, and with the box on her left as yet unoccupied, Villanelle enters the nest of red plush. The box is at once public and private. At the front, perched on one of the gilt chairs, with the scarlet-upholstered rail at chest level, Villanelle can see and be seen by everyone in the auditorium. If she leans forward past the partition, she can look into the front of the boxes on either side of her. With the house lights extinguished, however, each box will become a secret world, its interior invisible.

In the gloom of that unseen, secret world, she slips her bag from her shoulder and takes out a lightweight Ruger automatic pistol with an integrated Gemtech suppressor and inserts a clip of .22mm low-velocity rounds. Returning the weapon to the bag, she places it on the floor at the base of the partition separating her from the box to her left.

In the nine months following her rebirth as Villanelle, she killed two men. Each project was initiated by a one-word text from Konstantin, followed by the transmission of detailed background documents – film clips, biographies, surveillance reports, schedules – from sources unknown to her. Each planning period lasted about four weeks, in the course of which she was armed, informed of any logistical support she might expect, and provided with an appropriate identity.

The first target, Yiorgos Vlachos, had been buying radioactive cobalt-60 in Eastern Europe with a probable view to detonating a dirty bomb in Athens. She had put an SP-5 round through his chest as he changed cars in the port of Piraeus. The shot, taken with a Russian VSS at a range of 325 metres, had involved an all-night lie-up under a tarpaulin on a warehouse roof. Later, reliving the event in the safety of her hotel room, Villanelle felt an intense, heart-pounding exhilaration. The dry snap of the suppressed report, the distant smack of the impact, the collapsing figure in the scope.

The second target was Dragan Horvat, a Balkan politician who ran a human trafficking network. His mistake had been to take his work home with him, in the form of a pretty, heroin-addicted seventeen-year-old from Tblisi. Unaccountably, he had fallen in love with her, and taken to flying her on expensive shopping sprees in European capital cities. London was the couple's favourite weekend destination, and when Villanelle bumped into him in a Bayswater side street late one evening Horvat smiled indulgently. He didn't immediately feel the stab wound to the inner thigh that severed his femoral artery, and as he bled to death on the pavement his Georgian girlfriend watched him with spaced-out eyes, absently twisting the gold bracelet that he'd bought her that afternoon in Knightsbridge.

In between kills Villanelle lived in the Paris apartment. She explored the city, sampled the pleasures it had to offer, and enjoyed a succession of lovers. These affairs always took the same course: a heady pursuit, a devouring couple of days and nights, the abrupt termination of all contact. She simply vanished from their lives, as swiftly and as mystifyingly as she had entered them.

She ran in the Bois de Boulogne every morning, attended a ju-jitsu dojo in Montparnasse, and practised her marksmanship at an elite shooting club in Saint-Cloud. Meanwhile, unseen hands paid her rent and managed her trading activities, whose proceeds were paid into a current account at the Société Générale. 'Spend what you like,' Konstantin told her. 'But stay under the radar. Live comfortably but not excessively. Don't leave a trail.'

And she didn't. She made no surface ripple. Became part of that monochrome army of professionals who hurried from place to place, their solitude stamped into their gazes. What authority imposed the sentences of death that she executed, she didn't know. She didn't ask Konstantin, because she was certain that he wouldn't tell her, and in truth, she didn't really care. What mattered to Villanelle was that she had been chosen. Chosen as the instrument of an all-powerful organisation which had understood, just as she herself had always understood, that she was different. They had recognised her talent, sought her out, and taken her from the lowest place in the world to the highest, where she belonged. A predator, an instrument of evolution, one of that elite to whom no moral law applied. Inside her, this knowledge bloomed like a great dark rose, filling every cavity of her being.

Slowly, the auditorium of the Teatro Massimo begins to fill. Sitting back in her seat, Villanelle studies the programme, her face shadowed by the partition between her box and the next. The performance time arrives and the house lights dim, the audience hubbub fading to silence. As the conductor takes his bow, to warm applause, Villanelle hears a figure quietly take his place in the adjoining box. She doesn't turn, and as the curtain rises on the first act, leans forward to gaze with rapt attention at the stage.

Minute succeeds minute; time is slowed to a crawl. Puccini's music engulfs Villanelle, but does not touch her. Her consciousness is focused, in its entirety, on the unseen person to her left. She forces herself not to look, but senses his presence like a pulse, malign and infinitely dangerous. At moments, she feels a coldness at the nape of her neck, and knows that he is watching her. Finally the strains of the *Te Deum* die away, the first act ends, and the crimson and gold curtain falls.

As the house lights come up for the interval, and conversation swells in the auditorium, Villanelle sits motionless as if hypnotised by the opera. Then, without a sideways glance, she stands and leaves the box, noting with her peripheral vision the presence of two bodyguards who are lounging, bored but watchful, at the end of the corridor.

Moving unhurriedly into the vestibule, she makes her way to the bar and orders a glass of mineral water, which she holds but doesn't drink. At the far end of the room, she sees Leoluca Messina moving towards her. Pretending she hasn't seen him, she turns into the crowd, re-emerging near the entrance to the foyer. Outside, on the opera house steps, the heat of the day has not yet abated. The sky is rose-pink over the sea, a livid purple overhead. Half-a-dozen young men passing Villanelle whistle and make appreciative comments in the local dialect.

She returns and takes her place in her box moments before the curtain rises on the second act. Once again she makes a point of not glancing to her left at Greco; instead, she gazes fixedly at the stage as the opera unfolds. The story is a dramatic one. Tosca, a singer, is in love with the painter Cavaradossi, who has been falsely accused of aiding the escape of a political prisoner. Arrested by Scarpia, the chief of police, Cavaradossi is condemned to die. Scarpia, however, proposes a deal: if Tosca gives herself to him, Cavaradossi will be released. Tosca agrees, but when Scarpia approaches her, she seizes a knife and kills him.

The curtain falls. And this time, when Villanelle has finished applauding, she turns to Greco and smiles, as if seeing him for the first time. It is not long before there is a knock at the door of the box. It is one of the bodyguards, a heavyset man who enquires, not discourteously, if she would care to join Don Salvatore for a glass of wine. Villanelle hesitates for a moment and then politely nods her acceptance. As she steps into the corridor the second bodyguard looks her up and down. She has left her bag in the box, her hands are empty, and the Valentino dress clings to her lean, athletic form. The two men glance knowingly at each other. It is clear that they have delivered many women to their boss. The heavyset man gestures to the door of Greco's box. '*Per favore, Signorina . . .*'

He stands as she enters. A man of medium height in an expensively cut linen suit. A lethal stillness about him, and a smile that doesn't begin to reach his eyes. 'Excuse my presumption,' he says. 'But I couldn't help observing your appreciation of the performance. As a fellow opera lover I was wondering if I might offer you a glass of *frappato*? It comes from one of my vineyards, so I can vouch for its quality.'

She thanks him. Takes an exploratory sip of the cold wine. Introduces herself as Sylviane Morel.

'And I am Salvatore Greco.' There is a questioning note in his voice but her gaze does not flicker. It is clear to him that she has no idea who he is. She compliments him on the wine and tells him that it is her first visit to the Teatro Massimo.

'So what do you think of Farfaglia?'

'Superb. A fine actress and a great soprano.'

'I'm glad you like her. I was fortunate enough to assist, in a small way, with her training.'

'How wonderful to see your belief in her confirmed.'

'*Il bacio di Tosca.*'

'Excuse me?'

'*Questo é il bacio di Tosca.* "This is Tosca's kiss!" Her words when she stabs Scarpia.'

'Of course! I'm sorry, my Italian . . .'

'Is most accomplished, Signorina Morel.' Again, that icy half-smile.

She inclines her head in denial. 'I don't think so, Signor Greco.' Part of her is conducting the conversation, part of her is calculating ways and means, timing, evasion routes, exfiltration. She is face to face with her target, but she is alone. And this, as Konstantin has so often made clear, is how it will always be. No one else can be involved except in the most peripheral, disconnected way. There can be no backup, no staged diversion, no official help. If she's taken, it's the end. There will be no discreet official leading her from the cell, no waiting vehicle to speed her to the airport.

33

They talk. For Villanelle, language is fluid. Most of the time she thinks in French, but every so often she awakes and knows that she's been dreaming in Russian. At times, close to sleep, the blood roars in her ears, an unstoppable tide shot through with polyglot screams. On such occasions, alone in the Paris apartment, she anaesthetises herself with hours of web-surfing, usually in English. And now, she notes, she is mentally playing out scenarios in Sicilian-inflected Italian. She hasn't sought out the language, but her head echoes with it. Is there any part of her that is still Oxana Vorontsova? Does she still exist, that little girl who lay night after night in urine-sodden sheets at the orphanage, planning her revenge? Or was there only ever Villanelle, evolution's chosen instrument?

Greco wants her, she can tell. And the more she plays the well-born, impressionable young Parisienne with the wide-eyed gaze, the greater his desire grows. He's like a crocodile, watching from the shallows as a gazelle inches closer to the water's edge. How does it usually play out? she wonders. Dinner somewhere they know him well, with the waiters deferential and the bodyguards lounging at a neighbouring table, followed by a chauffeured drive to some discreet, old town apartment?

'Every first night, this box is reserved for me,' he tells her. 'The Greci were aristocrats in Palermo before the time of the Habsburgs.'

'In that case I consider myself fortunate to be here.'

'Will you stay for the final act?'

'With pleasure,' she murmurs, as the orchestra strikes up.

As the opera continues, Villanelle once again gazes raptly at the stage, waiting for the moment that she has planned. This comes with the great love duet, '*Amaro sol per te*'. As the final note dies away, the audience roars its applause, with cries of '*Bravi!*' and '*Brava Franca!*' echoing from every corner of house. Villanelle applauds with the others, and eyes shining, turns to Greco. His eyes meet hers, and as if on impulse, he seizes her hand and kisses it. She holds his gaze for a moment, and raising her other hand to her hair, unfastens the long, curved clip, so that the dark tresses fall to her shoulders. And then her arm descends, a pale blur, and her clip is buried deep in his left eye.

His face blanks with shock and pain. Villanelle presses the tiny plunger, injecting a lethal dose of veterinary-strength etorphine into the frontal lobe of his brain and inducing immediate paralysis. She lowers him to the floor, and glances around. Her own box is empty, and in the box beyond, an elderly couple are dimly visible, peering at the stage through opera glasses. All eyes are on Farfaglia and the tenor singing Cavaradossi, both standing motionless as wave after wave of applause breaks over them. Reaching over the partition, Villanelle recovers her bag, retires into the shadows, and takes out the Ruger. The double snap of the suppressed weapon is unremarkable, and the low-velocity .22 rounds leave barely a loose thread as they punch though Greco's linen jacket.

The applause is subsiding as Villanelle opens the door of the box, her weapon concealed behind her back, and beckons concernedly to the bodyguards, who enter and genuflect beside their employer. She fires twice, less than a second separating the silenced shots, and both men drop to the carpeted floor. Blood jets briefly from the entry wounds in the back of their necks, but the men are already dead, their brainstems shot through. For several long seconds, Villanelle is overwhelmed by the intensity of the killings, and by a satisfaction so piercing that it's close to pain. It's the feeling that sex always promises but never quite delivers, and for a moment she clutches herself, gasping, through the Valentino dress. Then slipping the Ruger into her bag and squaring her shoulders, she exits the box.

'Don't tell me you're leaving, Signorina Morel?'

Her heart slams in her chest. Walking towards her down the narrow corridor, with the sinister grace of a panther, is Leoluca Messina.

'Unfortunately, yes.'

'That's too bad. But how do you know my uncle?'

She stares at him.

'Don Salvatore. You've just come out of his box.'

'We met earlier. And now, if you'll excuse me, Signor Messina . . .'

He looks at Villanelle for a moment, then steps firmly past her and opens the door of Greco's box. When he comes out, a moment later, he is carrying a gun. A Beretta Storm 9mm, part of her registers as she levels the Ruger at his head.

For a moment they stand there unmoving, then he nods, his eyes narrowing, and lowers the Beretta. 'Put that away,' he orders.

She doesn't move. Aligns the fibre-optic foresight with the base of his nose. Prepares to sever a third Sicilian brainstem.

'Look, I'm glad the bastard's dead, OK? And any minute now, the curtain's going to come down and this whole place is going to be crowded with people. If you want to get out of here, put that gun away and follow me.'

Some instinct tells her to obey. They hurry through the doors at the end of the corridor, down a short flight of stairs, and into a crimson-upholstered passageway encircling the stalls. 'Take my hand,' he orders, and Villanelle does so. Coming towards them is a uniformed usher. Messina greets him cheerily, and the usher grins. 'Making a quick getaway, Signor?'

'Something like that.'

At the end of the passageway, directly below Greco's box, is a door faced in the same crimson brocade as the walls. Opening it, Messina pulls Villanelle into a small vestibule. He parts a blanket-like curtain and suddenly they are backstage, in the heavy half-dark of the wings, with the music, relayed by tannoy from the orchestra pit, blaring about them. Men and women in nineteenth-century costume swim out of the shadows; stagehands move with regimented purpose. Placing an arm round Villanelle's shoulder, Messina hurries her past racks of costumes and tables set with props, then directs her into the narrow space between the cyclorama and the brick back wall. As they cross the stage they hear a volley of musket-fire. Cavaradossi's execution.

Then more corridors, discoloured walls hung with fire extinguishers and instructions for emergency evacuation of the house, and finally they are stepping from the stage door onto the Piazza Verdi, with the sound of traffic in their ears and the livid purple sky overhead. Fifty metres away, a silver and black MV Agusta motorcycle is standing at a bollard on the Via Volturno. Villanelle climbs up behind Messina, and with a low growl of exhaust they glide into the night.

It's several minutes before they hear the first police sirens. Leoluca is heading eastwards, winding through side streets, the MV Agusta nervily responsive to the sharp twists and turns. At intervals, to her left, Villanelle catches a glimpse of the lights of the port and the inky shimmer of the sea. People glance at them as they pass – the man with the wolfish features, the woman in the scarlet dress – but this is Palermo; no one looks too closely. The streets narrow, with washing suspended above and the sounds and smells of family meals issuing through open windows. And then a dark square, a derelict cinema and the baroque facade of a church.

Rocking the bike onto its stand, Messina leads her down an alley beside the church, and unlocks a gate. They are in a walled cemetery, a city of the dead, with family tombs and mausoleums extending in dim rows into the night. 'This is where they'll bury Salvatore when they've dug your bullets out of him,' says Messina. 'And sooner or later, where they'll bury me.'

'You said you were happy to see him dead.'

'You've saved me the trouble of killing him myself. He was *un animale*. Out of control.'

'You'll take his place?'

Messina shrugs. 'Someone will.'

'Business as usual?'

'Something like that. But you? Who do you work for?'

'Does it matter?'

'It matters if you're going to come after me next.' He draws the squat little Beretta from his shoulder holster. 'Perhaps I should kill you now.'

'You're welcome to try,' she says, drawing the Ruger.

They stare at each other for a moment. Then, without lowering the weapon, she steps towards him, and reaches for his belt. 'Truce?'

The sex is brief and savage. She holds the Ruger throughout. Afterwards, placing her gun hand on his shoulder for balance, she wipes herself with the tail of his shirt.

'And now?' he says, watching her with awed repulsion, and noting how, in the half-light, the asymmetrical tilt of her upper lip makes her look not sensual, as he'd previously imagined, but coldly rapacious.

'Now you go.'

'Will I see you again?'

'Pray that you don't.'

He glances at her for a moment and walks away. The MV Agusta kicks into life with a snarl and fades into the night. Picking her way downhill between the tombs, Villanelle finds a small clearing in front of a pillared mausoleum. From the Fendi shoulder bag she takes a Briquet lighter, a crumpled blue cotton frock, a pair of wafer-thin sandals and a lingerie-fabric money belt. The money belt holds €500 in cash, an airline ticket, and a passport and credit card identifying her as Irina Skoryk, a French national born in Ukraine.

Quickly changing her clothes, Villanelle makes a pyre of the Valentino dress, all documents relating to Sylviane Morel, and the green contact lenses and brunette wig that she has been wearing. The fire burns briefly but intensely, and when there is nothing left she sweeps the ashes into the undergrowth with a cypress branch.

Continuing downhill, Villanelle finds a rusty exit gate, and a path leading down steps to a narrow lane. This gives onto a broader, busier road, which she follows westwards towards the city centre. After twenty minutes she finds what she has been looking for: a large wheeled garbage bin behind a restaurant, overflowing with kitchen waste. Pulling on the opera gloves she looks around her, and makes sure that she's unobserved. Then she plunges both hands into the bin, and pulls out half a dozen bags. Unknotting one, she thrusts the

Fendi shoulder bag and the Ruger into the stinking mess of clam shells, fish heads and coffee grounds. Returning the bag to the bin, she piles the others on top. Last to disappear are the gloves. The whole operation has taken less than thirty seconds. Unhurriedly, she continues walking westwards.

At 11 a.m. the following morning, agent Paolo Vella of the Polizia di Stato is standing at the bar of a cafe in the Piazza Olivella, taking coffee with a colleague. It has been a long morning; since dawn Vella has been manning the cordon at the main entrance to the Teatro Massimo, now a crime scene. The crowds, by and large, have been respectful, keeping their distance. Nothing has been officially announced, but all Palermo seems to know that Don Salvatore Greco has been assassinated. Theories abound, but the general assumption is that this is family business. There's a rumour that the hit was carried out by a woman. But there are always rumours.

'Will you look at that,' breathes Vella, all thoughts of the Greco murder temporarily banished. His colleague follows his gaze out of the cafe into the busy street, where a young woman in a blue sundress – a tourist, evidently – has paused to watch the sudden ascent of a flight of pigeons. Her lips are parted, her grey eyes shine, the morning light illuminates her close-cropped hair.

'Madonna or whore?' asks Vella's colleague.

'Madonna, without question.'

'In that case, Paolo, too good for you.'

He smiles. For a moment, in the sun-dazed street, time stands still. Then as the pigeons circle the square, the young woman continues on her way, long limbs swinging, and is lost in the throng.

2

Villanelle sits in a window seat in the south wing of the Louvre art gallery in Paris. She is wearing a black cashmere sweater, leather skirt, and low-heeled boots. Winter sunshine pours through the vaulted window, illuminating the white marble statue in front of her. Life-sized, and entitled *Psyche Revived by Cupid's Kiss*, it was carved by the Italian sculptor Antonio Canova in the final years of the eighteenth century.

It's a beautiful thing. Psyche, awakening, reaches upwards to her winged lover, her arms framing her face. Cupid, meanwhile, tenderly supports her head and breast. Every gesture speaks of love. But to Villanelle, who has been watching the visitors come and go for an hour now, Canova's creation suggests darker possibilities. Is Cupid luring Psyche into a sense of false security so that he can rape her? Or is it Psyche that's sexually manipulating him, by pretending to be passive and feminine?

Unaccountably, passers-by seem to take the sculpture at its romantic face value. A young couple imitate the pose, laughing. Villanelle watches closely, notes how the girl's gaze softens, how the flutter of her eyelashes slows, how her smile turns to a shy parting of the lips. Turning the sequence over in her mind like a phrase in a foreign language,

Villanelle files it away for future use. Over the course of her twenty-six-year lifespan she has acquired a vast repertoire of such expressions. Tenderness, sympathy, distress, guilt, shock, sadness . . . Villanelle has never actually experienced any such emotions, but she can simulate them all.

'Darling! There you are.'

Villanelle looks up. It's Anne-Laure Mercier. Late as usual, with wide apologetic grin. Villanelle smiles, they air-kiss, and stroll towards the Café Mollien on the gallery's first-floor landing. 'I've got a secret to tell you,' Anne-Laure confides. 'And you mustn't tell a *soul*.'

Anne-Laure is the closest thing that Villanelle has to a friend. They met, rather absurdly, at the hairdresser. Anne-Laure is pretty, extrovert and more than a little lonely, having exchanged life at a busy public relations firm for marriage to a wealthy man sixteen years her senior. Gilles Mercier is a senior functionary at the Treasury. He works inordinately long hours, and his greatest passions are his wine cellar and his small but important collection of nine-teenth-century ormolu clocks.

But Anne-Laure wants to have fun, a commodity sadly lacking in the life she shares with Gilles and his clocks. Right now, before they've even reached the curving stone staircase up to the restaurant, she's pouring out the details of her latest affair, with a nineteen-year-old Brazilian dancer at the Paradis Latin cabaret.

'Just be careful,' Villanelle warns her. 'You have a lot to lose. And most of your so-called friends would go straight to Gilles if they thought you were playing around.'

'You're right, they would.' Anne-Laure sighs, and links her arm through Villanelle's. 'You're so sweet, you know that? You never judge me, and you're always so concerned.'

Villanelle squeezes the other woman's arm. 'I care about you. I don't want to see you hurt.'

In truth, it suits Villanelle's purposes to spend time with Anne-Laure. She's well-connected, with an insider's access to the finer things of life. Haute couture shows, tables at the best restaurants, membership of the best clubs. Besides which she's undemanding company, and two women together attract far less attention than a woman on her own. On the negative side Anne-Laure is sexually reckless, and it can only be a matter of time before some indiscretion is brought to Gilles's attention. When that happens, Villanelle doesn't want to give the impression that she's complicit in his wife's infidelity. The last thing she needs is the hostile attention of a senior public servant.

'So how come you're not shorting the Nikkei Share Index or whatever it is that day-traders do?' Anne-Laure asks, when they are finally installed at a table.

Villanelle smiles. 'Even super-capitalists need a day off. Besides, I wanted to hear about this new guy of yours.' She looks around her at the shining silver and glassware, the flowers, the paintings, the golden wash of the lights. Outside, beyond the tall windows, the sky has faded to a snow-laden grey, and the Carousel Gardens are almost deserted.

As they eat, and Anne-Laure talks about her new *amour*, Villanelle makes attentive noises. But her mind is elsewhere. Fine-living and designer clothes are all very well, but it's months now since the Palermo operation, and she badly needs to feel her heart race with the prospect of action.

More than that, she wants confirmation that she's valued, that the organisation regards her as a prime asset.

She can still see, half a world away, the grim sprawl of the Dobryanka remand centre. Was it worth it? Konstantin had asked her. Throwing her life away to avenge her father, himself a man who'd gone to the bad. Put like that, of course, it wasn't worth it. But given her time again, she knew that she'd act exactly as she'd acted that night.

Her father had been a close-quarter battle instructor before he'd started freelancing for the Brothers' Circle. And although Boris Vorontsov hadn't been the ideal parent, given to whoring and heavy drinking, and dumping Oxana in the orphanage whenever he went away on active service, he was her flesh and blood, and all she had after her mother's death.

There hadn't been many birthday or New Year presents, but her father had taught her to defend herself, and more. There had been memorable days in the forest, wrestling in the snow, shooting at tin cans with his old Makarov service pistol, and lopping through birch-trunks with his Spetsnaz-issue machete. She'd hated the machete at first, finding it heavy and unwieldy, but he'd taught her how it was all in the timing. That if you got it right, the weight of the blade and the arc of the swing did the job for you.

She'd found out easily enough who killed him. Everyone knew; that was the point. Boris had tried, clumsily, to defraud the Brothers, and they'd shot him and left his body in the street. The following evening Oxana walked into the Pony Club on Ulitsa Pushkina. The three men she was looking for were standing near the bar, drinking and laughing, and when she sauntered up to them, smiling suggestively, they fell silent. In her army-surplus jacket and supermarket jeans she didn't look much like a *shlyukha*, a whore, but she was certainly acting like one.

Oxana stood there for a moment in front of them, looking from face to face with taunting, amused eyes. Then she dropped into a crouch, her arms reaching back between her shoulder blades for the machete in its webbing holster, and drove upwards through her knees as her father had taught her. Half a kilo of titanium-finished steel blurred the air, the chisel-edge passing unchecked through the first man's throat before burying itself deep below the second man's ear. The third man's hand dived to his waistband, but too late: Oxana had already let go of the machete and drawn the Makarov. Around her, she was vaguely aware of panicked breathing, suppressed screams, people backing away.

She shot him through the open mouth. The report was deafening in the enclosed space, and for a moment he just stood there staring at her, blood and brain-matter spilling from a gaping white flap of bone at the back of his head. Then his legs went, and he hit the floor beside the first man, who was somehow still on his knees, a desperate, dregs-of-the-milkshake rasp issuing from the bubbling gash beneath his chin. The third man wasn't finished yet, either. Instead, he was lying in a foetal position in the spreading red lake, his feet working feebly and his fingers plucking at the machete embedded in the angle of his jaw.

Oxana watched them, annoyed at their failure to die. It was the kneeling man who really infuriated her, making that sick, Strawberry McFlurry noise. So she knelt beside him, drenching her Kosmo jeans in blood. His gaze was failing, but the eyes still held a question. 'I'm his daughter, you cunt,' she whispered and, pressing the Makarov's barrel to the nape of his neck, squeezed the trigger. Again, the detonation was appallingly loud, and the man's brains went everywhere, but the sucking noise stopped.

'*Chérie!*'

She blinks. The restaurant swims back into focus. 'Sorry, I was miles away . . . What did you say?'

'Coffee?'

Villanelle smiles at the waiter hovering patiently at her side. 'Small espresso, thank you.'

'Honestly, sweetie, sometimes I wonder where you go in these daydreams of yours. Are you seeing someone you haven't told me about?'

'No. Don't worry, you'd be the first to know.'

'I'd better be. You can be so mysterious at times. You should come out with me more often, and I don't mean shopping or fashion shows. I mean . . .' She draws a fingertip down the frosted stem of her champagne flute. 'More *fun* stuff. We could go to Le Zéro Zéro or L'Inconnu. Meet some new people.'

In her bag, Villanelle's phone buzzes. A single word textmessage: CONNECT.

'I have to go. Work.'

'Oh, please, Vivi, you're impossible. You haven't even had your coffee.'

'I'll do without.'

'You're so *boring*.'

'I know. Sorry.'

Two hours later Villanelle is sitting in the study of her rooftop apartment in the Porte de Passy. Beyond the plate-glass window the sky is cold steel.

The email contains a few lines of text about skiing conditions in Val-d'Isère, and half-a-dozen JPEG images of the resort are attached. Villanelle extracts the password and accesses the payload of compressed data embedded in the images. It is a face, shot from different angles. A face she memorises like the text. The face of her new target.

Thames House, the headquarters of the British security service MI5, is on Millbank, in Westminster. In the northern-most office on the third floor, Eve Polastri is looking down at Lambeth Bridge and the wind-blurred surface of the river. It's 4 p.m. and she has just learnt, with mixed feelings, that she is not pregnant.

At the next terminal, her deputy Simon Mortimer replaces his teacup in its saucer. 'Next week's list,' he says. 'Shall we run through it?'

Eve takes off her reading glasses and rubs her eyes. Wise eyes, her husband Niko calls them, although she's only twenty-nine, and he's almost ten years older. She and Simon have been working together for a little over two months. Their department, known as P3, is a subsection of the Joint Services Analysis Group, and its function is to assess the threat to 'high-risk' individuals visiting the UK, and if necessary to liaise with the Metropolitan Police with a view to providing specialist protection.

It's in many ways a thankless task, as the Met's resources are not infinite, and specialist protection is expensive. But the consequences of a poor judgement call are catastrophic.

47

As her former head of section Bill Tregaron once said to her, before his career went into freefall: 'If you think a live extremist preacher's a headache, wait until you have to deal with a dead one.'

'Tell me,' Eve says to Simon.

'The Pakistani writer, Nasreen Jilani. She's speaking at the Oxford Union on Thursday week. She's had death threats.'

'Plausible?'

'Plausible enough. SO1 have agreed to put a team on her.'

'Go on.'

'Reza Mokri, the Iranian nuclear physicist. Again, full protection.'

'Agreed.'

'Then there's the Russian, Kedrin. I'm not so sure about him.'

'What aren't you sure about?'

'How seriously we should take him. I mean, we can't ask the Met to babysit every crackpot political theorist who shows up at Heathrow.'

Eve nods. With her make-up-free complexion and shoulder-length hair gathered in a scrappy up-do, she looks like someone for whom there are more important things than being thought pretty. She might be an academic, or an assistant in the better sort of bookshop. But there's something about her – a stillness, a fixity of gaze – that tells another story. Her colleagues know Eve Polastri as a hunter, a woman who will not readily let go.

'So who requested protection for Kedrin?' she asks.

'Eurasia UK, the group which organised his visit. I've run checks, and they're—'

'I know who they are.'

'Then you'll know what I mean. They look more cranky than dangerous. All this stuff about the mystical bonds between Europe and Russia, and how they should unite against the corrupt, expansionist USA.'

'I know. It's pretty wild. But they've got no shortage of supporters. Including in the Kremlin.'

'And Viktor Kedrin's their poster boy.'

'He's the ideologist. The face of the movement. Charismatic figure, apparently.'

'But not at immediate risk in London, surely?'

'Maybe, maybe not.'

'I mean, who would he be at risk from? The Americans aren't crazy about him, obviously, but they're not going to call in a drone strike on High Holborn.'

'Is that where he's going to be staying?'

'Yes, at somewhere called The Vernon.'

Eve nods. 'I suppose you're right. We don't need to trouble Protection Command with Mr Kedrin. But I think I might go to his talk – I assume he's addressing the Eurasia UK faithful at some point?'

'The Conway Hall. Friday week.'

'Good. Keep me posted.'

Simon inclines his head in assent. Although only in his twenties, he has the arch solemnity of a metropolitan vicar.

Keying in her identification code, Eve calls up the HST, or High Security Threat list. Circulating among friendly intelligence services, including on–off allies like the Russian FSB and the Pakistani CID, this is a database of known international contract killers. Not local enforcers or fly-in-fly-out shooters, but top-echelon assassins with political clients and price tags affordable only by the seriously wealthy. Some of the entries are lengthy and detailed, others are no more than a code name harvested in the course of surveillance or interrogation.

For over two years now Eve has been building up her own file of unattributed killings of prominent figures. A case she constantly returns to is that of Dragan Horvat, a Balkan politician. Horvat was an exceptionally nasty piece of work, implicated in human trafficking and much else besides, but that didn't save Bill Tregaron when Horvat was murdered in Central London on his watch. Relieved of his post, Bill was seconded to GCHQ, the government listening centre at Cheltenham, and Eve, previously his deputy, became head of section at P3.

Horvat was killed on a trip to London with his girlfriend, a seventeen-year-old heroin addict from Tblisi named Irema Beridze. Officially, he was in London as a member of a high-ranking trade delegation; in truth, he and Irema spent most of their time shopping. They had just left a Japanese restaurant in a poorly lit side street in Bayswater when a hurrying figure bumped hard into Horvat, almost knocking him down.

In a cheerful mood, well lubricated by sake, Horvat was initially unaware that he had been stabbed. Indeed, he apologised to the disappearing figure before becoming aware of the warm blood pumping from his groin. Open-mouthed with shock, he sunk to the pavement, one hand clamped uselessly to his severed femoral artery. It took him less than two minutes to die.

Irema was still standing there, shivering and uncomprehending, when a party of Japanese businessmen left the restaurant quarter of an hour later. Their English was imperfect, hers non-existent, and it was a further ten minutes before anyone called the emergency services. Irema was profoundly traumatised, and initially insisted that she could remember nothing about the attack. But patient questioning by an officer from the Metropolitan Police's SO15 Branch, assisted by a Georgian interpreter, eventually elicited a single key fact. Dragan Horvat's killer was a woman.

Professional female assassins are very rare indeed, and since joining the service Eve has been aware of just two. For some years, according to the HST file, the FSB used a woman named Maria Golovkina to execute overseas hits. A member of Russia's small-bore pistol squad at the Athens Olympics, Golovkina is thought to have been trained in covert assassination at the Spetsnaz base in Krasnodar. There's also an entry in the file for a Serbian hitwoman, attached to the notorious Zemun clan, named Jelena Markovic.

Neither could have killed Horvat, for the simple reason that by the time the politician met his end in London both were dead. Golovkina had been found hanged in a hotel wardrobe in Brighton Beach more than a year earlier, and Markovic had predeceased her by four months, blown to shreds by a car bomb in Belgrade. So if Irema Beridze was right, it meant that there was a new female assassin abroad. And this interests Eve very much indeed.

Why, she isn't completely sure. Perhaps because she can't imagine taking a human life herself, she is fascinated by the notion of a woman for whom killing is unexceptional. Someone who could get up in the morning, make coffee, choose what to wear, and then go out and cold-bloodedly put a total stranger to death. Did you have to be some kind of anomalous, psychopathic freak to do that? Did you have to be born that way? Or could any woman, correctly programmed, be turned into a professional executioner?

Since taking over P3 from Bill, Eve has conducted a discreet but exhaustive search of the live case files for any further suggestion of female involvement in an assassination, and has flagged two references. The first involves the shooting in Germany of Aleksandr Simonov, a Russian business oligarch suspected of funding Chechen and Dagestani militants as part of a deal relating to oil and gas concessions. The assassin, who fired a burst of six rounds from an FN P90 sub-machine gun into Simonov's chest outside the Frankfurt headquarters of the AltInvest Bank, was wearing despatch-riders' waterproofs and a full-face motorcycle helmet, and raced away on a machine later identified as a BMW G650Xmoto. Of the dozen or so onlookers questioned afterwards, two stated that they 'had the impression' that the shooter was a woman.

The other case, the close-up slaying in Sicily of a Mafia boss named Salvatore Greco, is apparently non-political. Local innuendo attributes the slaying, directly or indirectly, to the dead man's nephew, Leoluca Messina, who has since assumed the leadership of the Greco clan. But there has also been speculation in the press about an accomplice, the so-called 'woman in the red dress'. According to the investigators of the DIA, the Direzione Investigativa Antimafia, Greco was found dead in a private box at the Teatro Massimo in Palermo, following an opera performance. He had been shot in the heart at close range with two low-velocity .22 rounds. His two bodyguards were also found dead on the floor of the box, despatched with single shots to the base of the skull.

Leoluca Messina is known to have been at the theatre that night, and a witness has described seeing him in the bar shortly before curtain-up, talking to a striking dark-haired woman in a red dress. It appears that they were not sitting together, but CCTV footage shows Messina leaving the theatre via the stage door shortly after the final curtain. A couple of paces behind him is a blurred figure: a woman in a red dress, dark hair swinging around her shoulders. Her face is invisible, masked by the opera programme that she's holding up as if to fan herself.

Which, Eve reflects, is certainly no accident. The woman is well aware that the CCTV camera is there. But the really strange detail is one that the DIA have not made public. Before Greco was killed, he was immobilised with a lethal tranquilliser apparently delivered via a custom-made device that was found buried in his left eye. A photograph of this device is in the online case-file, along with details of its inner workings. It's a sinister-looking thing: a curved and hollowed steel spike containing an inner reservoir and armed with a tiny plunger.

Why was it necessary to incapacitate Greco in this way before shooting him? It's a question that's nagged Eve for some time, and she's no nearer finding an answer than she was on the day that she first read the file. Given that the assassination took place in an essentially public location, wouldn't it have made sense to get it over with quickly? Why, with discovery possible at any moment, would the killer want to drag things out?

Eve is still pondering this question when she arrives back at the flat in Finchley a few minutes before eight o'clock. Her husband, Niko, is not there; he's gone ahead to the bridge club where he instructs three evenings a week. He's left a *pierogi* – a Polish dumpling dish – in the oven, which Eve retrieves gratefully. She's not much of a cook and hates having to prepare meals from scratch when she arrives back after a long day at Thames House.

As she eats, she watches the eight o'clock news summary on the BBC. There's a warning of a cold front coming in from the east ('Make sure your boilers are serviced!'), an overwhelmingly bleak piece about the economy, and an imported clip of a rally in Moscow, where an impassioned, bearded figure is addressing an attentive crowd in a snow-whitened square. A blurry caption identifies him as Виктор Кедрин.

Eve leans forward in her seat, a forkful of *pierogi* suspended in her hand. Despite the poor image-quality, Viktor Kedrin's magnetism is palpable. She strains to hear his words behind the commentator's voice-over, but the clip cuts to a story of an orphaned kitten adopted by a chihuahua.

When she's finished eating, Eve exchanges her work clothes for jeans, a sweater and a zip-up windproof jacket. The result is unsatisfactory, but she can't be bothered to give it more thought. She looks around the flat, from the waist-high stacks of books in the narrow front hall to the clothes hanging from the drying-rack in the kitchen. If and when I get pregnant, she tells herself, we're going to need somewhere bigger. For a moment, she allows her thoughts to linger on the airy red-brick mansions in Netherhall

Gardens, just five minutes' walk away. A first-floor apartment in one of those would be perfect. And about as likely to come into her and Niko's possession as Buckingham Palace. The combined salaries of a Security Services officer and a teacher just didn't stretch to that sort of place. If they wanted somewhere larger, they'd have to move further out. Barnet, perhaps. Or Totteridge. She rubs her eyes. Even the thought of moving is exhausting.

She zips up her windproof. The club is ten minutes away, and as she walks, she thinks of that cold front coming in from the east. It seems to promise not just ice and snow, but menace.

It's a tournament night at the West Hampstead Bridge Club, and the place is filling fast. The game room is laid out with folding baize-topped tables and stackable plastic chairs. It's warm after the chill of the streets, and there's an animated buzz of conversation round the bar.

Eve spots Niko Polastri, her husband, straight away. He's playing a practice hand with three beginners, his gaze attentive, his movements economical. Even at a distance Eve can see from their body language how anxious the novices are to impress him. A woman with teased blonde hair leads a card, and Niko regards it for a moment before picking it up and returning it to her with a grave smile. She looks confused for a moment, then her hand flies to her mouth and everyone at the table laughs.

Niko has the gift of imparting knowledge with grace and humour. In the North London school where he teaches maths he's popular with the pupils, who are generally acknowledged to be a tough bunch. At the club, where he is one of four senior instructors, the members compete openly for his approval, with even the flintiest veterans melting at a word of praise for a stylishly executed finesse, or a contract made against the odds.

Eve met Niko four years ago, when she first joined the club. At the time she was less interested in improving her bridge-playing than in finding a social life disconnected from the intense, inward-looking hive of Thames House. A social life that would hopefully feature an attractive, intelligent man. In her mind's eye she saw a suave figure, his features not quite discernible, leading her up a broad flight of steps to a smart West End restaurant.

The bridge club, whose members had an average age somewhere north of fifty, did not deliver such a man. Had she wished to meet retired accountants and widowed dentists, it would have been just the place, but attractive single men under forty were thin on the ground. Niko wasn't there when she first presented herself; she and a couple of other prospective members were attended to by Mrs Shapiro, the blue-haired club secretary.

Dispirited by the experience, she was in two minds about going back the next week. But she went, and this time Niko was there. A tall man with patient brown eyes and the moustache of a nineteenth-century cavalry officer, he took charge of Eve from the moment she arrived, squiring her to a table, summoning two more players, and partnering her without comment for half-a-dozen hands. Then, dismissing the others, he faced her over the green baize table.

'So, Eve. Good news, or not-so-good news?'

'Not-so-good news first, I think.'

'OK. Well, you understand the basics of the game. You learnt as a child?'

'My parents both played, yes.'

'And you like, very much, to win.'

Eve meets his gaze. 'Is it that obvious?'

'To others, maybe not. You like to play the *myszka*, the mouse. But I see the fox.'

'Is that good?'

'It could be. But you have faults.'

'A faulty fox?'

'Exactly. If you're going to play a strategic game, you need to know very early on where all the cards are. To do this, you need to concentrate harder on your opponents' play. You need to remember the bidding, and count every suit.'

'Right.' She digested this for a moment. 'So what's the good news?'

'The good news is that there's a very nice pub just five minutes away.'

She laughed. They were married later that year.

Eve's bridge partner tonight is a young guy, perhaps nineteen, one of a trio of students from Imperial College who joined the club in the autumn. He's got a slightly mad-scientist look about him, but he's a ferociously good player, and at the West Hampstead that's what counts.

After her initial uncertainty, Eve has come to look forward to her evenings here. Some of the members are her parents' age and even, in one or two cases, her grandparents'. But the standard of play is fierce, and after a rigorous day at Thames House she appreciates the idea of intellectual challenge for its own sake.

At the end of the evening she thanks her partner. They've finished fourth overall, a good result, and he grins a little awkwardly and shuffles off. At the entrance Niko helps her into her zip-up waterproof jacket as if it was a Chanel coat, a tiny act of chivalry that does not go unnoticed by other female members, who glance at Eve enviously.

'So how was your day?' she asks him, linking her arm tightly through his as they make their way back towards the flat. It's just started to snow, and she blinks as the flakes touch her face.

'The Year 11 boys would have a better understanding of differential calculus if they didn't all stay up until two in the morning playing Final Attrition 2. Or maybe not. How about you?'

She hesitates. 'I've got a problem for you. I've been trying to figure it out all day.'

Niko knows what she does, and while he never presses her for information Eve often thinks how useful a mind like his would be to her employers. At the same time the thought of him walking the featureless corridors of Thames House fills her with horror. It's her world, but she wouldn't want it to be his.

After leaving Cracow University with a Master's degree in Pure and Applied Mathematics, Niko took off round Europe in a battered van with a friend named Maciek. Living and sleeping in the van, the pair travelled from tournament to tournament – bridge, chess, poker, anything offering a cash prize – and after eighteen months on the road, retired with over a million zloty between them. Maciek spent his share in less than a year, mostly on the girls at the Pasha Lounge on Warsaw's Ulitsa Mazowiecka. Niko headed for London.

'Tell me,' he says.

'OK. Three dead men on the floor of a theatre box, after a performance. Two bodyguards and a Mafia don. All shot. But the don has been tranquillised first. Paralysed by an immobilising agent injected into one eye. What's the story? Why was he not just shot like the bodyguards?'

Niko is silent for a minute. 'Who was killed first?'

'I'm assuming the bodyguards. The shooter, thought to be the don's nephew, used a silencer. Low-calibre weapon at point-blank range.'

'Body shots?'

'The don, yes. The bodyguards, back of the neck. No mess. Very professional.'

'And the syringe, or whatever. The immobilising agent. What do we know about that?'

'I'll show you.'

She takes a photocopy of a photograph from her bag. They stop for a moment in a whirl of snowflakes beneath a street light.

'Nasty-looking thing.' He blows snow from his moustache. 'But clever. And perhaps it wasn't the nephew. Is there a woman involved?'

She stares at him. 'What makes you say that?'

'The killer's first problem is how to get past the bodyguards with a weapon. These are going to be tough, experienced guys.'

'OK.'

'But this, on the other hand . . .' He holds up the photocopy. 'They're not going to give this a second look.'

'How come?'

He reaches into his coat pocket, and takes out a pen. 'Look, if I draw a retaining wire which attaches here, and snaps into place there, what do we have?'

Eve stares at the limp photocopy. 'Oh for fuck's sake. How can I have missed that?' Her voice is a whisper now. 'It's a hairclip. A woman's fucking hairclip.'

Niko looks at her. 'So, is there a woman involved?'

In the business-class lounge at Charles de Gaulle airport, Villanelle checks her messages. A coded text confirms that Konstantin will meet her at the La Spezia cafe in Gray's Inn Road in London at 2 p.m. as arranged. Returning her phone to her bag she sips her coffee. The lounge is warm, with smoothly moulded seating in restful shades of white and taupe; the walls are flecked with illuminated leaf-shapes. Beyond the plate-glass exterior wall the tarmac, slush and sky are a barely distinguishable grey.

Villanelle is travelling on a false passport as Manon Lefebvre, the co-author of a French investment newsletter. Her cover story is that she is in London to talk to an online publisher interested in setting up a partnership. She looks professionally anonymous in a mid-length trenchcoat, narrow jeans and ankle boots. She's wearing no make-up, and despite the season, grey-lensed acetate sunglasses; airports attract photographers and, increasingly, law-enforcement profes-sionals armed with facial recognition software.

An Air France steward appears in the lounge and directs the business-class passengers to their flight. Villanelle has reserved the front aisle seat in the waiting Airbus, and although she makes a point of not meeting his eye, she can tell that the man in the window seat, currently flicking through an inflight magazine, is determined to engage her in conversation. She ignores him, and taking out a 4G tablet and earphones, is soon immersed in a video clip.

The clip shows, in slow motion, the contrasting terminal performances of two handgun rounds when fired into a block of clear ballistics gelatin, a testing medium designed to simulate human tissue. One round is Russian, one American. Both are jacketed hollow point, designed to deliver massive kinetic shock and remain within a target's body rather than passing through. Knowing that she's likely to be operating in a busy urban environment, this information is of interest to Villanelle. She's going to want a one-shot, lights-out kill. She can't risk the possibility of collateral damage.

She frowns, torn between the two hollowpoint rounds. The Russian round expands on entry, its jacket peeling back like the petals of a flower as it blasts through flesh and bone. The US round, by contrast, doesn't deform but tumbles nose over point, tearing a devastating wound cavity as it goes. Both have their very considerable merits.

'Could I ask you to switch off your device, Mademoiselle?'

It's the stewardess, chic in her dark-blue tailored suit.

'Of course.' Villanelle smiles coolly, blanks the screen and takes out the earphones.

'Good movie?' asks her companion, seizing his chance.

She noticed him earlier, in the business-class lounge. Late thirties and implausibly good-looking, like a designer-dressed matador.

'Actually, I was shopping.'

'For yourself?'

'No, for someone else?'

'Someone special?'

'Yes. It's going to be a surprise.'

'Lucky him.' He levels a dark-brown gaze at her. 'You're Lucy Drake, aren't you?'

'Excuse me?'

'Lucy Drake? The model?'

'Sorry, no.'

'But . . .' He reaches for the inflight magazine, and pages through it until he reaches a fragrance advertisement. 'That's not you?'

Villanelle looks at the page. It's true, the model does look uncannily like her. But Lucy Drake's eyes are a piercing green. The fragrance is called *Printemps*. Spring. Villanelle takes off her sunglasses. Her own eyes are the frozen grey of the Russian midwinter.

'Forgive me,' he says. 'I was mistaken.'

'It's a compliment. She's lovely.'

'She is.' He holds out his hand. 'Luis Martín.'

'Manon Lefebvre.' She looks down at the magazine, now on the armrest between them. 'How did you know that model's name, if you don't mind me asking?'

'I'm in the business. My wife and I own an agency, Tempest. We've got divisions in Paris, London, Milan and Moscow.'

'And this Lucy Drake is on your books?'

'No, I think she's with Premier. She's not working so much any more.'

'Really?'

'She wants to act, apparently. And she thinks the more editorial and advertising she does, the less chance she has of being taken seriously.'

'So does she have talent?'

'She has talent as a model, which is very much rarer than you might think. As an actress . . .' He shrugs. 'But then people so often undervalue their real talents, wouldn't you say? They dream of being something they can never be.'

'You're Spanish?' asks Villanelle, deflecting the personal questions that she senses coming.

'Yes, but I spend very little time in Spain. Our main residences are in London and Paris. Do you know London?'

She considers. Did six weeks' brutal unarmed combat training in the Essex marshes count? A fortnight spent hurtling round hairpin bends on the evasive driving course at Northwood? A week learning to pick locks with a retired burglar on the Isle of Dogs?

'A little,' she says.

The stewardess is back with champagne. Martín accepts, Villanelle asks for mineral water.

'You should think of modelling,' he says. 'You have the cheekbones, and the fuck-you stare.'

'Thank you very much.'

'It's a compliment, believe me. What do you do?'

'Financial stuff. Much less glamorous, I'm afraid. So . . . was your wife a model?'

'Elvira? Yes, originally she was. A very successful one. But these days I deal with the clients, and she runs the back office.'

The conversation takes its predictable course. Villanelle is guarded on the subject of her alter-ego Manon Lefebvre, and presses Martín for details about Tempest. With two glasses of Veuve Clicquot drunk and a third half-empty, he's only too happy to talk about himself, while simultaneously plying Villanelle with a stream of increasingly flirtatious compliments.

For a moment she wonders if he's a plant from MI5, or France's external intelligence service, the DGSE. But she didn't book the London flight; instead she took a taxi hailed at random outside the Galeries Lafayette on the Boulevard Haussmann, and paid cash for her ticket when she got to the airport. Basic counter-surveillance measures, including a last-second pull-off into a service station on the A1 autoroute, told her that she wasn't followed from Paris. And Martín was in the business-class lounge before her, already checked in. Most importantly, her instincts – highly tuned when it's a question of her own survival – tell her that this man is not playing a role. That he really is the over-groomed seducer that he appears to be. The joke about narcissistic types like Martín is that they always think they're in control – at work, in conversation, during sex.

Her thoughts drift to that night in Palermo. Say what you like about Leoluca Messina, he didn't have control issues. In fact he was perfectly happy to let her fuck him while she was holding a cocked and loaded Ruger. In its way, the whole episode was quite romantic.

Konstantin is sitting in front of the cafe counter, facing the door and Gray's Inn Road. The *Evening Standard* is open in front of him at the sports page, and he's sipping a cappuccino. When Villanelle walks in, stamping snow from her boots, he looks up, his gaze vague, and nods her to a seat opposite him. The downbeat welcome robs the moment of its potential drama; no one looks up at the young woman in the thrift-shop coat and knitted beanie. She orders a cup of tea, and the pair begin an inaudible conversation. Were anyone to attempt audio surveillance they would find their efforts frustrated by the low-fi snarl of the sound system and the steamy hiss and cough of the Gaggia coffee machine.

For thirty minutes, as customers come and go, they discuss logistics and weaponry in fast, idiomatic Russian. Konstantin tests Villanelle's plan to destruction, throwing up objection after objection, but finally concedes its workability. He orders a second cappuccino, and stirs his cup meditatively.

'Palermo worried me,' he tells her. 'What you did, driving through the city at midnight on the back of Messina's motorcycle, that was reckless. Things could have gone badly wrong.'

'I improvised. I was in control throughout.'

'Listen to me, and listen well. You are never completely safe. And you can never fully trust anyone.'

'Not even you?'

'Yes, Villanelle, you can trust me. But part of you should always be mistrustful, questioning and attuned to danger. Part of you *shouldn't* fully trust me. I want you to survive, OK? Not just because you're so good at what you do, but . . .'

He stops, annoyed that his concern for her has momentarily become personal. From the first, in that hut by the Chusovaya river, he has sensed the cross-currents of sex and death swirling beneath her icy surface. Known that the implacable hunger that drives her could also destroy her. For a moment, she looks almost vulnerable.

'Go on.'

65

His eyes rake the busy cafe. 'Look, right now, no one knows for sure that you even exist. But what happens this week could change everything. The British are a vengeful people. If you give them half a chance, their security services will come after you with everything they've got, and they will not back off.'

'So it's important, this action?'

'It's vital. Our employers don't take these decisions lightly, but this man must be eliminated.'

With a finger, she traces a V in spilt tea on the melamine surface of the table. 'I sometimes wonder who they are, these employers of ours.'

'They're the people who decide how history is to be written. We are their soldiers, Oxana. Our job is to shape the future.'

'Oxana is dead,' she murmurs.

'And Villanelle must survive.'

She nods, and even in the winter dimness of the cafe he can see that her eyes are shining.

Later, high above South Audley Street in Mayfair, she looks westwards. Beyond the floor-to-ceiling window the sky is umber in the twilight, and the trees are grey. Snowflakes drive silently against the plate glass.

The top-floor apartment is registered in the name of a corporate finance group. There's a TV suite and a state-of-the-art sound system, which Villanelle will not use, and a fully provisioned kitchen, which she will leave only slightly depleted. For the next forty-eight hours she will spend much of her time here in the bedroom, sitting as now in a white leather Charles Eames chair, waiting. There are moments when she would welcome the sting of loneliness. Instead, she feels a level blankness, neither happy nor unhappy. She senses a rising of the tide, an echo of the action to come. Konstantin will do his part, but in the end there will just be her, and Kedrin, and the moment.

She touches a finger to her mouth, to the faint ridge of the scar. She was six when her father brought Kalif home. A hunting dog rejected by its previous owner, the animal attached itself devotedly to Oxana's mother, who was already gravely ill. Oxana wanted Kalif to love her, too, and one day she climbed onto the steel-framed bed in which her mother passed her increasingly pain-wracked days and nights, and pressed her face close to the dog, which was curled up on the thin blanket. Baring sharp teeth in a vicious snarl, Kalif struck out at her.

There was a lot of blood, and Oxana's torn lip, stitched without anaesthetic by a medical student from a neighbouring apartment, was slow to heal. Other children stared at her, and by the time the wound ceased to be noticeable Oxana's mother was dead, her father was in Chechnya and Oxana herself had been consigned to the tender mercies of the Sakharov Orphanage.

Villanelle could easily have her upper lip remodelled by a plastic surgeon, so that it curves into the perfect bow that nature intended, but she hasn't done so. The scar is the last vestige of her former self, and she can't quite bring herself to erase it.

From nowhere she feels a morbid crawl of desire. Rolling onto her side on the white leather, she presses her thighs together and clasps her arms across her small breasts. For several minutes she lies like this, her eyes closed. She recognises it, this hunger. Knows that it will tighten its grip unless satisfied.

She showers, dresses, and slicks back her hair. The lift conveys her soundlessly to the ground floor, and the street. She blinks as the first whirling snowflakes find her face. Cars pass with a faint hiss of tyres, but there aren't many people on foot, except a prostitute in a faux leopardskin coat and platform heels waiting on the corner of Tilney Street, patiently eyeing the forecourt of the Dorchester Hotel. Walking northwards, navigating on impulse, Villanelle turns from South Audley Street into Hill Street, then through an archway into a narrower road leading to a square so small it's almost a courtyard. One side is taken up by a brightly illuminated gallery window, beyond which a private view is taking place. There's a single spotlit object in the window: a stuffed weasel on a plinth, strewn with bright, multicoloured cupcake sprinkles.

Villanelle stares at it. The sprinkles look like multiplying bacilli. The installation, or sculpture or whatever it is, conveys nothing to her.

'Are you coming in?'

The woman – late thirties, black cocktail dress, wheat-blonde hair pulled back in a chignon – is leaning out of the glass door of the gallery, holding it half-closed to keep the cold air at bay.

Shrugging, Villanelle enters the gallery, losing sight of the woman almost immediately. The place is packed with prosperous-looking invitees. A few are looking at the paintings on the walls but most are facing inwards, conversing in tight groups as catering staff edge between them with canapés and bottles of cold Prosecco. Sweeping a glass from one of the trays, Villanelle positions herself in a corner. The paintings seem to have been reproduced from blown-up press photographs and blurry snatches of film. Anonymous, faintly sinister groupings, several with the faces blacked out. A man in a velvet-collared coat is standing in front of the nearest painting, a study of a woman in the back seat of a car, her shocked features lit by photoflash, her arm raised against the invading lenses of the paparazzi.

Studying the man's expression – the faint frown of concentration, the unwavering gaze – Villanelle duplicates it. She wants to be invisible, or at least unapproachable, until she's finished her drink.

'So what do you think?'

It's the woman who invited her in. The man in the velvet-collared coat moves away.

'Who is she, in the painting?' Villanelle asks.

'That's the point, we don't know. She could be a film star arriving at a premiere, or a convicted murderer arriving for sentencing.'

'If she was a murderer she'd be handcuffed, and she'd arrive at the court in an armoured van.'

The woman looks at Villanelle, takes in the chic Parisian crop and the Balenciaga biker jacket, and smiles. 'Are you speaking from experience?'

Villanelle shrugs. 'She's some burnt-out actress. And she's probably wearing no pants.'

There's a long moment's silence. When the woman speaks again, the register of her voice has subtly changed. 'What's your name?' she asks.

'Manon.'

'So, Manon. This event will take another forty minutes, and then I'm closing the gallery. After that I think we should go and eat yellowtail sashimi at Nobu in Berkeley Street. What do you say?'

'OK,' says Villanelle.

Her name is Sarah, and she had her thirty-eighth birthday a month ago. She's talking about conceptual art, and Villanelle is nodding vaguely but not really listening. Not to the words, anyway. She likes the rise and fall of Sarah's voice, and she's touched, in an abstract sort of way, by the tiny age-lines around her eyes, and by her seriousness. Sarah reminds her, just a little, of Anna Ivanovna Leonova, a teacher at Industrialny District secondary school, and the only adult, except her father, to whom she's ever formed a real, unsimulated attachment.

'Is that good?' Sarah asks.

Villanelle nods and smiles, examining a pearlescent sliver of raw fish before crushing it, pensively, between her teeth. It's like eating the sea. Around them, soft lights touch surfaces of brushed aluminium, black lacquer and gold. There's a whisper of music; conversation rises and falls. Sarah's lips form words, and Sarah's eyes meet hers, but it's Anna Ivanovna's voice that Villanelle hears.

For two years the teacher nurtured her charge's exceptional academic gifts, and showed endless patience for her graceless, barely socialised behaviour. Then one day, Anna Ivanovna wasn't there. She'd been attacked and sexually assaulted while waiting for a late bus home from school. In hospital the teacher was able to describe her assailant to the police, and they arrested an eighteen-year-old former pupil named Roman Nikonov, who had boasted of his intention to show the unmarried teacher 'what a real man felt like'. But the police botched the forensics, and in the end Nikonov was released on a technicality.

'Manon!' She feels Sarah's cool hand take hers. 'Where are you?'

'Sorry. Miles away. You remind me of someone.'

'Someone?'

'A teacher at my school.'

'I hope she was nice.'

'She was. And she looked like you.' Except that she didn't. She was really nothing like Sarah. Why had she thought that? Why had she *said* that?

'Where did you grow up, Manon?'

'St Cloud, outside Paris.'

'With your parents?'

'With my father. My mother died when I was seven.'

'Oh my God. That's awful!'

Villanelle shrugs. 'It was a long time ago.'

'So what did she . . .'

'Cancer. She was just a couple of years younger than you.' Cover stories are part of Villanelle's life now. Clothes she puts on, takes off, and hangs up for next time.

'I'm so sorry.'

'Don't be.' Withdrawing her hand from Sarah's, Villanelle opens the menu. 'Look at this! Wild strawberry sake jelly. We *have* to have some.'

She's always regretted that it was too dark to see Roman Nikonov's expression when she castrated him in the woods by the Mulyanka river. But she remembers the moment.

71

The smell of the mud, and of the exhaust from his Riga moped. The pressure of his hand on her head, forcing her to her knees. The throttled screams, carrying far out over the water, as she pulled out the knife and hacked his balls off.

Sarah lives in a tiny flat over the gallery. As they walk back there, hand in hand, they leave dark footprints in the new snow.

'OK, I get the paintings, but what's *that*?' Villanelle asks, pointing to the cryptic installation in the gallery window.

Sarah keys a code into the keypad by the door. 'Well . . . the stuffed weasel was a present, given to me as a joke. And the sprinkles were in the kitchen. So I put them together. Quite fun, don't you think?'

Villanelle follows her up a narrow flight of stairs. 'So it doesn't mean anything at all?'

'What do you think?'

'I don't think anything. I don't care.'

'So what do you—'

Villanelle half-turns and pins her to the wall, silencing her with her mouth. It's a moment that's been inevitable, but Sarah's still taken by surprise.

Much later, she wakes to see Villanelle sitting upright in bed, her lean upper body silhouetted against the first dawn light. Reaching for her, Sarah runs a hand down her arm, feels the hard curves of her deltoid and bicep. 'What exactly was it that you said you did?' she asks wonderingly.

'I didn't say.'

'Are you going?'

Villanelle nods.

'Will I see you again?'

Villanelle smiles, and touches Sarah's cheek. Dresses quickly. Outside, in the little square, there's virgin snow, and silence. Back at the South Audley Street apartment, she kicks off her clothes and is asleep within minutes.

When she awakes it's past noon. In the kitchen there's a half-full cafetière of Fortnum & Mason's Breakfast Blend coffee, still warm. Several sizeable carrier bags stand by the front door, where Konstantin has left them.

She checks the goods. A pair of tortoiseshell-framed glasses with pale-grey lenses. A parka with a fur-trimmed hood. A black polo-neck sweater, a plaid skirt, black woollen tights and zip-up boots. She tries it all on, walks around, accustoms herself to the look. The outfit needs wearing in, so she drinks a cup of the cooling coffee, leaves the apartment building, and makes her way across Park Lane to Hyde Park.

Again, that umber sky, against which the avenues of leafless beeches and oaks are a darker grey-brown. It's early afternoon but the light is already ebbing. Villanelle walks fast along the slush-banked paths, hands in pockets, head down. There are other walkers, but she barely glances at them. At intervals statues loom out of the dimness, their outlines blurred with encrusted snow. On a balustraded bridge across the Serpentine she pauses for a moment. Beneath a cracked and starred pane of ice the water is a lightless black. A realm of darkness and forgetting to which, on days like this, she feels herself almost hypnotically drawn.

'Tempting, isn't it?'

Villanelle turns, amazed to hear her thoughts so precisely echoed. He's about thirty, lean-featured, in a well-cut tweed coat with the collar turned up.

'I wasn't planning on doing any swimming.'

'You know what I mean. "To sleep: perchance to dream . . ."' His eyes are steady, and as dark as the frozen waterway.

'You admire Shakespeare?'

He wipes snow off the balustrade with his sleeve, and shrugs. 'He's a good companion in a war zone.'

'You're a soldier?'

'Used to be.'

'And now?'

He lifts his gaze to the distant glow of Kensington. 'Research, you might say.'

'Well, good luck with that . . .' She rubs her ungloved hands together, and blows into them. 'The light's going. And so should I.'

'Home?' The broken smile suggests they're sharing a private joke.

'That's right. Goodbye.'

He raises a hand. 'See you around.'

Hunching into her parka, she walks away. Just some fucked-up weirdo hitting on her. Except that he wasn't. With that lethal English courtliness of his, he's both more and less threatening than that. And familiar, somehow. Is it possible that she's seen him before, perhaps in the course of the counter-surveillance exercises that she performs, almost subconsciously, wherever she goes? Is he MI5?

Angling sharply southwards, she glances back at the bridge. The man has disappeared, but she still senses his presence. Heading northwards for the nearest exit she performs a cleaning run, designed to shake off any tail that she might have picked up. No one follows, no one changes direction, no one speeds up to match her pace. But if they're serious, whoever they are, they'll have a primary team foot-following, and a secondary team on static surveillance, ready to latch on if she burns the primaries.

Turning eastwards, Villanelle walks along Bayswater Road towards Marble Arch. Not racing, but fast enough to make any tail pick up his or her speed. She stops briefly at a bus stop as if resting her legs, discreetly checking the area for anyone in the calculatedly drab plumage of the professional pavement artist. There's no one obvious, but then if she had one of MI5's A4 teams locked on to her, there wouldn't be.

Forcing herself to breathe steadily, she makes for the Marble Arch underpass network. With its multiple exits, it's a good place to expose and lose a tail. Descending the steps at Cumberland Gate she surfaces beside the Edgware Road, and hovers in a sports shop entrance, watching the reflection of the underpass exit in the plate-glass window. No one glances at her, no one breaks step. Strolling to the Marble Arch entrance, she speed-walks the hundred-odd metres through the underpass, cuts back on herself by Speaker's Corner, and makes for the tube station. On the westbound Central Line platform she lets the first two trains pass, scanning the platform for stay-behinds. The line's busy, and there are several possibles. A young woman in a grey windproof jacket, carrying a backpack. A bearded guy in a reefer jacket. A middle-aged couple holding hands.

Stepping onto the third train, she travels as far as

Queensway, and then just as the doors are closing, squeezes out between them. Crossing the platform, she returns eastbound to Bond Street, surfaces, and hails a taxi in Davies Street. For the next ten minutes she sends the driver on a circuitous route through Mayfair. A grey BMW follows them for a time, but then turns eastwards on Curzon Street with an irritable growl. A minute later a black Ford Ka appears in the wing-mirror, and three turn-offs later is still there. As they coast into Clarges Mews, a choke-point, Villanelle hands the driver a fifty-pound note and issues swift instructions. Thirty seconds later the taxi drifts to a halt, blocking the road, and the engine dies. As Villanelle slips out of a rear door, she hears the angry blare of the Ka's horn, but no one follows her down the narrow, brick-walled passageway, and when she doubles back five minutes later, the mews is deserted.

And perhaps, she tells herself later in the South Audley Street apartment, no one was following me anyway. What would be the point? If the UK Intelligence Services know who and what I am, then it's all over. There won't be an arrest, just a visit from a Special Forces action team, probably E Squadron, and cremation in a municipal waste incinerator. This, according to Konstantin, is the British way, and nothing that Villanelle has seen of the British gives her the slightest reason to doubt him.

But the E Squadron scenario is not going to happen, and with a smooth effort of will, she erases the apprehensions prompted by the afternoon's encounter. Curled like a panther on the white leather Eames chair, she raises a glass of pink Alexandre II Black Sea champagne to the fading light. The wine is neither distinguished nor expensive, but it's a symbol of everything that in her other, earlier life she could never have dreamed of.

And it suits her mood. She's in lockdown now, her focus already narrowing to the moment-by-moment details of the next day's action. Anticipation rises through her, as sharp and effervescent as the bubbles prickling to the surface of the champagne, and with it the ache of the hunger that never completely goes away. She coils and uncoils on the white leather. Perhaps she'll go out and have some more sex. It will help kill a few hours.

Eve groans. 'What time is it?'

'Six forty-five,' murmurs Niko. 'Like every day at this time.'

Eve buries her face in the warm valley between his shoulder blades, clinging to the last vestiges of sleep. The strangulated coughing of the espresso machine overlays the measured tones of Radio 4's *Today* programme. She's decided, during the night, to put a SO1 Protection team on Viktor Kedrin.

'Coffee's done,' Niko says.

'OK. Give me a couple of minutes.'

Returning from the bathroom, she smacks her shin, not for the first time, on the low, glass-fronted fridge that he bought a month earlier on eBay.

'Shit, Niko, *please*. Do we have to have this . . . thing here?'

He rubs his eyes. 'Not if you don't want milk in your coffee in the morning, *myszka*. Besides, where else would you like me to put it? There's no room in the kitchen.'

Ensuring that the blind is down – it has a habit of shooting up without warning – Eve lifts her nightdress over her head, and reaches for her underwear. 'I'd argue that we don't need a medical standard refrigeration unit to cool one little milk jug. And if there's no room in the kitchen, it's because it's full of all your stuff.'

'Ah, suddenly it's all *my* stuff?'

'OK, Swedish cookbooks? That solar-powered microwave . . .'

'They're Danish. And that microwave is going to save us money.'

'When? This is London NW3. There isn't any frigging sun for eleven months of the year. Either we get rid of some of your stuff, or we move somewhere bigger. And a lot less nice.'

'We can't move.'

She dresses quickly. 'Why not?'

'Because of the bees.' He knots a dark-brown tie over a silver-grey shirt.

'Niko, please. Don't get me started on those fucking bees. I can't go into the garden, the neighbours are terrified of being stung to death . . .'

'One word, *myszka*. Honey. This summer, we could harvest fifteen kilos per hive. I've spoken to the deli, and—'

'Yes, I know it all makes sense in the future. Your five-year economic plan. But it's the here and now we have to deal with. I can't live like this. I can't think straight.'

They cross the tiny landing, stepping over a stack of back issues of *Astronomy Now* and an ancient, dented cardboard box marked *Oscilloscope Testing Equipment/ Cathode Ray Tube*, and descend the stairs.

'I think the First Directorate is working you too hard, *Evochka*. You need to chill out.' He checks the knot of his tie in the hall mirror, and gathering up a pile of exercise books from a shelf, shunts them into a battered Gladstone bag. 'You are going to make it back in time for the tournament at the club tonight, aren't you?'

'Should do.' The calculation being that with an SO1 team on Kedrin, she won't feel duty-bound to attend his lecture, or political rally, or whatever it is.

Eve pulls on her coat, and Niko sets the state-of-the-art alarm that Thames House has thoughtfully provided. The front door closes, and hand in hand, their breath vaporous, they make their way through the half-light of morning towards Finchley Road tube station.

In the P3 office at Thames House, Simon Mortimer looks inscrutable as he puts down the receiver. 'Unless you can come up with a specific reason for changing your mind on Kedrin, it's no go,' he tells Eve. 'Too short notice.'

Eve shakes her head. 'That's ridiculous. SO1 could easily have a team in place at half a day's notice. Is the foot-dragging coming from our end, or theirs?'

'Ours, as far as I can tell. There's hesitation to deploy SO1 on the basis of, um . . .'

'Of what?'

'The phrase used was "female intuition".'

She stares at him. 'Seriously?'

'Seriously.'

She closes her eyes.

'On the positive side, you have made your concern known. Your ass, if I may refer to it as such, is covered.'

'I suppose you're right. But really, "female intuition"?' What I said in my memo was that I was concerned that I'd underestimated the potential threat to Kedrin.'

'What exactly made you change your mind?'

On her screen, Eve calls up an article from *Izvestiya*. 'OK, this is from a speech he gave last month in Ekaterinburg. I'm translating. "Our sworn enemy, which we will fight to the death, and to which we will never surrender, is American hegemony in all its forms. Atlanticism, liberalism, the deceitful" – he actually says snake-like – "ideology of human rights, and the dictatorship of the financial elite."'

'Pretty standard stuff, surely?'

'Agreed. But there's a huge tranche of the Russian and former Sov-bloc population who see him as a kind of messiah. And messiahs don't have a long shelf life. They're too dangerous.'

'Well, let's hope he says his piece at the Conway Hall and pushes off fast.'

'Let's hope.' She rubs her eyes. 'I suppose I ought to go. Don't much feel like it, but . . .' She exits the *Izvestiya* page. 'Simon, can I ask you something?'

'Of course.'

'Do you think I should do something about, you know, the way I dress? That female intuition comment makes me worried I'm sending the wrong message?'

He frowns. 'Well, I know you're not even slightly like that. And as we're so often reminded, discretion is the keynote of the Thames House style. But I don't think there'd be any harm in your, perhaps, venturing a teensy bit further afield than the Marks and Spencer's Classic and Indigo ranges.' He looks at her a little nervously. 'What does your husband think?'

'Oh, Niko lives in a fashion universe all of his own. He teaches maths.'

'Ah.'

'I just don't want to see this department's authority undermined, Simon. We make serious decisions, and we need to be taken seriously.'

He nods. 'Are you busy tomorrow afternoon?'

'Not specially. Why?'

'Well, I don't want to perpetuate any stereotypes here, but perhaps you and I could go shopping?'

The Vernon Hotel is a six-storey edifice faced with grey stone on the north side of High Holborn. Its clientele is, for the most part, as anonymous as its frontage, so reception manager Gerald Watts is happy to give his attention to the strikingly attractive young woman standing before him. She's wearing a fur-trimmed parka, and the eyes that meet his from behind the grey-tinted glasses are bright and direct. Her accent, with its hint of France and suggestion of Eastern Europe (after five years at the Vernon's front desk Gerald considers himself something of an expert in these matters), is charmingly fractured.

Her name, he discovers when he takes her credit card details, is Julia Fanin. She's not wearing a wedding ring; absurdly, this pleases him. Proffering her key-card to Room 416 he allows their fingers to touch. Is it his imagination, or does he detect a flicker of complicity? Indicating with a raised hand that one of his assistants take her valise and show her to her room, he watches the easy sway of her hips as she walks towards the elevator.

By the time that Eve arrives at Red Lion Square, it's 7.45. Inside the Conway Hall the crowd is about two hundred strong. The majority of those who have come to hear Viktor

Kedrin speak are already seated in the Main Hall; a few stand chatting against the wood-panelled walls, while others have found their way up to the gallery. Most are men, but there are a few couples here and there, and several younger women in T-shirts printed with Kedrin's portrait. And there are other more enigmatic figures, male and female, whose predominantly black clothing is imprinted with slogans which might be musical, mystical, political or all three.

Looking around her, Eve feels a little out of place, but not threatened. The hall is filling fast, and the various tribes seem content to coexist. If the individuals present have anything in common, it is perhaps that they are outsiders. Kedrin's audience is a coalition of the disenfranchised. Climbing the stairs to the gallery, she finds a seat at the front on the right-hand side, overlooking the stage and the lectern, and with a rush of guilt, realises that she hasn't called Niko to tell him that she can't make it to the bridge tournament. She searches her bag for her phone.

She doesn't tell him where she is, just that she can't come, and as always he's understanding. He never questions her about her work, her absences or her late nights. But she can tell that he's disappointed; it's not the first time he's had to apologise for her at the club. I must make it up to him, she tells herself. His patience isn't infinite, nor should it have to be. Perhaps we could go to Paris for a weekend. Take the Eurostar, stay in a little hotel somewhere and walk around the city hand in hand. It must be so romantic in the snow.

In the hall, the lights flicker and dim. On the stage a

ponytailed man walks to the lectern and adjusts the microphone.

'Friends, I greet you. And I apologise if my English is not so good. But it gives me pleasure to be here tonight, and to introduce my friend and colleague from St Petersburg State University. Ladies and gentlemen . . . Viktor Kedrin.'

Kedrin is an imposing figure, broad and bearded, in a battered corduroy jacket and flannel trousers. There's applause as he walks out, and a few cheers. Taking her phone from her bag, Eve grabs a shot of him at the lectern.

'It's cold outside,' Kedrin begins. 'But I promise you, it's colder in Russia.' He smiles, his eyes dead-leaf brown. 'So I want to talk to you about the spring. The Russian spring.'

Rapt silence.

'In the nineteenth century there was a painter named Alexei Savrasov. A great admirer, as it happens, of your John Constable. Naturally, like all the best Russian artists, Savrasov succumbed to alcohol and despair and died penniless. But first, he created a very fine series of landscape paintings, the best known of which is called *The Rooks Have Come Back*. It's a very simple painting. A frozen pond. A distant monastery. Snow on the ground. But in the birch trees, the rooks are building their nests. Winter is dying, spring is coming.

'And this, my friends, is my message to you. *Spring is coming*. In the Russian heartland, there is a yearning for change. And I feel the same thing in Europe. A longing to throw off the dictatorship of capitalism, of degenerate liberalism, of America. A longing to reclaim an older world of Tradition and the Spirit. So I say to you, *join us*. Leave the US to their pornography, their blood-sucking corporations and their empty consumerism. Leave them to their Reign of Quantity. Together, Europe and Russia can build a new Imperium, true to our ancient cultures, true to the old beliefs.'

Eve scans the ranks of the audience. Sees the rapt gazes, the mute nods of agreement, the desperate yearning to believe in the golden age that Kedrin promises. In the centre of the front row is a young woman in a black sweater and plaid skirt. She is a few years younger than Eve, and beautiful, even at a distance. On impulse, Eve raises her phone, and surreptitiously zooming in on the woman's face, photographs her. She catches her in profile, lips parted, gazing fervently up at Kedrin.

The speech gathers pace. Kedrin recalls another who dreamt of a new imperium – a thousand-year Reich, no less – but dismisses the Nazis for their crude racism and lack of higher consciousness. He makes an exception of the Waffen-SS, from whose rigorous idealism, he says, much can be learned. This is too much for one audience member, a middle-aged man who stands up and starts shouting incoherently at the stage.

Within seconds, two figures in quasi-military clothing appear from the shadows at the back of the hall, grab the man, and half-lead him, half-drag him towards the exit. A half-minute later, to desultory cheers, they return without him.

Kedrin smiles beatifically. 'There's always one, no?'

In all, he speaks for about an hour, setting out his mystical, authoritarian vision for the northern hemisphere. Eve is appalled but fascinated. Kedrin is charismatic, and satanically persuasive. That he will make true believers out of those assembled here tonight, she is in no doubt. He is not yet well known in Europe, but in Russia he commands a growing following, and has a small army of dedicated street fighters ready to do his will.

'And so my friends, I finish as I started, with that simple message. Spring is coming. Our day is dawning. The rooks have come back. Thank you.'

As one, the audience rises to its feet. As they cheer, stamp their feet, and applaud, Kedrin stands at the lectern, unmoving. Then, with a small bow, he leaves the stage.

Slowly, as Eve watches from the gallery, the hall empties. The spectators have a dazed look, as if waking from a dream. After a couple of minutes, accompanied by the ponytailed master of ceremonies and flanked by the two foot soldiers who ejected the protester, Kedrin appears in the auditorium. He is quickly surrounded by admirers, who take it in turn to address a few words to him and shake his hand. The woman from the front row waits on the outskirts of the group, a faint smile touching her sharp, cat-like features. *If I dressed like that I'd look like a librarian,* Eve muses. *So how come this little fascist princess gets to look like Audrey Hepburn?*

Kedrin's certainly registered her, and gives her a glance as if to say: *wait, just let me finish with these people and you'll have my full attention.* Soon, watched with barely suppressed amusement by the shaven-headed foot soldiers, the two of them are deep in conversation. Her body language – the head fetchingly tilted, the neat little breasts out-thrust – makes her availability unambiguously clear. But eventually she settles for shaking his hand, pulls on her parka, and vanishes into the night.

Eve is one of the last to depart the hall. She waits outside at a nearby bus stop, and when Kedrin and his party leave the building, she follows them at a discreet distance. After a couple of minutes the four men turn into an Argentinian steak restaurant in Red Lion Street, where they are clearly expected.

Deciding to call it a night, Eve makes for Holborn tube station. It's gone 9.30, and she's too late for the bridge tournament. But she'll get to the club in time to grab herself a large vodka and cranberry juice and watch Niko play a few hands. She needs to wind down. One way and another, it's been a weird day.

At a little after 9.45, when she's satisfied that the Russians are settled in, Villanelle moves away from the doorway from where she's been watching the steak house, and takes a back route to the hotel. As she moves through the lobby towards the lifts, her face shadowed by her fur-trimmed hood, she directs a smile and a brief flutter of her leather-gloved fingers at the reception desk, where Gerald Watts is still on duty.

Letting herself into Room 416, Villanelle opens the valise, takes out a packet of surgical gloves, and exchanges a pair for the leather ones she's wearing. Then, from a sealed polythene bag, she takes a micro-transmitter the size of a fingernail, and a pinch of Blu-Tack. Placing this in the pocket of her parka, she leaves the room and takes the stairs up to the fifth floor, where she seems to straighten a picture on the wall outside Room 521. This done, she continues upwards to the sixth floor, where the stairs terminate in an exit to the roof. It's unlocked, and stepping outside she conducts a quick reconnaissance of the area, noting the placement of chimney stacks and fire-escape ladders. Then, without hurry, she returns to the fourth floor.

Back in her room she switches on an iPod-sized UHF receiver, and inserts one of the in-ear headphones. Nothing, as she expected, just a faint, ambient hiss. Pocketing the receiver, leaving one ear-bud trailing, she takes a water-proof case from the valise. Inside, each component lying in its bed of customised foam, is the weapon she ordered from Konstantin: a polymer-bodied CZ 75 9mm handgun and an Isis-2 suppressor. Villanelle prefers a lightweight action on a combat weapon, and the CZ's trigger-pull weight has been adjusted to two kilos for double-action firing, and one kilo for single action.

Hotel-room assassination, she knows, is a complex science. Taking down the target is easy; it's doing so swiftly, silently and without collateral damage that's difficult. There must be no recognisable gunshot report, no scream of alarm or pain, no bullets smacking through plasterboard partition walls, or worse, through the guests on the other side of them.

So after attaching the suppressor, Villanelle loads the Czech handgun with Russian-made *Chernaya Roza* – Black Rose – hollowpoint rounds. These are constructed with an oxidised copper jacket whose six sections, on impact, peel back like petals. This slows penetration, initiates a massive and incapacitating shockwave, and causes enhanced disruption of tissue along the wound path. For a 9mm round, the Black Rose's stopping power is unequalled.

Villanelle waits, her breathing steady. Visualises and re-visualises the coming course of events. Replays every conceivable scenario. Through the headphones, she hears hotel guests bid each other goodnight, snatches of laughter, doors closing. It's more than an hour and a half before she hears what she's been waiting for: voices speaking Russian.

'Come in for five minutes. I've got a bottle of Staraya Moskva. We need to run over arrangements for tomorrow.'

Villanelle considers. The drunker they all are, the better. But she can't leave it too late. She hears murmurs of assent, and the sound of the door closing.

Again, Villanelle waits. It's past 1 a.m. when the security team finally, and noisily, leaves the room. But how drunk is Kedrin? Will he remember the wide-eyed young woman he met at the Conway Hall? She picks up the hotel phone and dials Room 521. A slurred voice answers. '*Da?*'

She answers in English. 'Mr Kedrin? Viktor? It's Julia. We spoke at the lecture. You said to call you later. Well . . . it's later.'

Silence. 'Where are you?'

'Here. At the hotel.'

'OK. I gave you my room number, yes?'

'Yes. I'll come up.'

She puts on the parka. The valise is now empty except for a clear plastic evidence bag. Opening this, Villanelle shakes its contents into the valise, which she then stows in the wardrobe. The evidence bag goes into the inside pocket of her parka. Then, after a last look around the room, she leaves, holding the CZ 75 by the suppressor so that the body of the handgun is up her sleeve.

Outside Room 521, she taps lightly on the door. There's a pause, and it opens a few inches. Kedrin is flushed, his hair awry, his shirt open halfway to the waist. His eyes narrow as he examines her.

'Can I come in?' she asks, tilting her head and looking up at him.

He bows, semi-ironically. Ushers her in with a vague, sweeping gesture. The room is similar to Villanelle's own, but larger. An ugly gilt chandelier hangs from the ceiling. 'Take off your coat,' he says, sitting down heavily on the bed. 'And get us a drink.'

She slips off her parka and drops it into an armchair, the CZ 75 concealed in the sleeve. A side table holds an empty bottle of Staraya Moskva vodka and four used glasses. Villanelle checks the fridge. In the freezer there's a plastic half-bottle of duty-free Stolichnaya. Uncapping the bottle, she pours a liberal amount into two of the glasses, and meeting his gaze, hands him one.

'A toast,' he says blearily, his eyes dropping to her breasts. 'We must have a toast. To love. To beauty!'

Villanelle smiles. 'I drink to our ruined home . . .' she begins, speaking Russian. 'And to life's evils, too . . .'

He stares at her for a moment, his expression at once surprised and melancholy, and continues the Akhmatova poem. 'I drink to the loneliness we share.' He throws back the vodka. 'And I drink . . .'

There's a sound like a snapping stick, and Kedrin is dead. Blood jets briefly from the entry wound beside his left nostril.

'. . . I drink to you,' murmurs Villanelle, completing the couplet as she pulls the bedclothes over him. Quickly, she pulls on the parka and makes for the door. As she's leaving the room, she finds herself face to face with one of Kedrin's pet thugs. He's broad-shouldered, scowling, and smells of cheap cologne.

'Ssshh,' hisses Villanelle. 'Viktor's sleeping.'

The eyes narrow in the skull-like head. Some instinct tells him that something is wrong. That he's fucked up. He tries to look past her, and realises far too late that the Glock 19 that he collected from the driver this morning is in his shoulder holster, not in his hand. Villanelle puts two rounds through the base of his nose, and as his knees go, catches the front of his flight jacket and swings him back through the door of the room. He falls backwards, hitting the monogrammed hotel carpet like a ton of condemned beef.

She briefly considers dragging the body out of view, but it will take more time than it will save. Then the phone in the room starts ringing, and she knows she has to get out. Making for the stairs she passes Skull-Head's colleague and Ponytail, hears them running to Kedrin's room. One look inside the door and they're after her, pounding along the corridor.

Villanelle races up the stairs to the sixth floor, continues upwards, and bursts out into the night. The roof is virgin white, and a blizzard of snow swirls around her as she bolts the stairwell door. Visibility is no more than a few feet. She has perhaps fifteen seconds start.

The door splinters and the lock flies outwards. The two men come out fast, breaking left and right respectively, leaving the door swinging in the icy wind. The roof is deserted. Footsteps lead from the stairwell to a balustrade, beyond which is whirling darkness.

Suspecting a trap, the two men duck behind a chimney stack. Then, very slowly, the younger man leopard-crawls across the snowy roof to the balustrade, peers over, and beckons cautiously to Ponytail. There, just visible, is Villanelle, with her back to them, the parka whipping around her body in the wind. She appears to be watching the chimney stack.

Both men discharge their weapons, and seven suppressed headshots tear through the parka hood. When the slight figure doesn't fall they freeze; there's an instant of terrible comprehension, and then their heads twitch in near unison as Villanelle squeezes off two shots from the fire escape behind them.

Like lovers, the two men fold into each other. And stepping up from the fire-escape ladder, unknotting the sleeves of her parka from the flue-pipe, Villanelle watches them die. As always, it's fascinating. There can't be much brain-function left after a Black Rose round has bloomed inside your cerebellum, clawing its way through your memory, instincts and emotions, but somehow, some spark lingers on. And then, inevitably, dims.

Standing there on the rooftop, in her cage of snow, Villanelle feels the longed-for power-surge. The feeling of invincibility that sex promises, but only a successful killing truly confers. The knowledge that she stands alone at the whirling heart of events. And looking around her, with the dead men at her feet, she sees the city resolved into its essential colours. Black, white and red. Darkness, snow and blood. Perhaps it takes a Russian to understand the world in those terms.

That Saturday is, without exception, the worst day of Eve Polastri's life. Four men shot dead on her watch, an A-grade

91

assassin on the loose in London, her MI5 superiors incandescent, the Kremlin no less so, a COBRA group convened, and – it goes without saying – her Thames House career fucked.

When the office ring to tell her that Viktor Kedrin has been found shot dead in his hotel room, she's still in bed. At first she thinks that she's going to faint, and then, staggering to the bathroom, and finding the corridor blocked by Niko's bicycle, she vomits all over her bare feet. By the time Niko reaches her, she's crouched on the floor in her nightdress, ash-grey and shaking. Simon rings while Niko is sitting with her in the kitchen. They agree to meet at the Vernon Hotel. Somehow, she manages to get dressed and drive there.

There's quite a crowd in Red Lion Street, held at bay by a barrier of crime-scene tape and two police constables. The senior investigating officer at the scene is DCI Gary Hurst. He knows Eve, and hurries her into the hotel, away from the probing camera lenses. In the reception area, he directs her to a banquette, pours her a cup of sugary tea from a Thermos flask, and watches as she drinks it.

'Better?'

'Yeah. Thanks, Gary.' She closes her eyes. 'God, what a shit-storm.'

'Well, it's a colourful one. I'll say that.'

'So what have we got?'

'Four dead. Shot at close range, all headshots, definitely a pro job. Victim one, Viktor Kedrin, Russian, university professor, found dead in his room. With him, victim two, late twenties, looks like hired muscle. On the roof, victims three and four. We think three is Vitaly Chuvarov, supposedly a political associate of Kedrin's, but almost certainly with organised crime connections. Four is more muscle. All armed with Glock 19s except for Kedrin. The pair on the roof discharged seven shots between them.'

'Must have picked up the weapons here.'

The DCI shrugs. 'Easily done.'

'Suggests they were expecting trouble.'

'Maybe. Maybe they just feel happier if they're carrying. Do you want to get suited up and go upstairs? The other Thames House guy's waiting for you up there.'

'Simon?'

'Yeah.'

'Sure. Where do I change?'

'Staging area that way.' He points. 'I'll be up in a minute.'

In the staging area Eve is handed a white Tyvek coverall, a mask, gloves and bootees. When she is finally suited up, dread floods through her. She's seen plenty of photographs of gunshot victims, but never any actual corpses.

She copes, though, and with Simon standing businesslike and imperturbable beside her, makes herself remember the details. The raised, greyish rims of the entry wounds, the thin trails of blackened blood, the faraway expressions. Kedrin, his sightless eyes directed at the ceiling, has a slight frown on his face, as if he's trying to remember something.

'You did your best,' says Simon.

She shakes her head. 'I should have insisted. I should have made the right decision in the first place.'

He shrugs. 'You made your concerns known. And you were overruled.'

She's about to answer when DCI Hurst calls her name and beckons to her from the top of the stairs.

'Thought you'd like to know. Julia Fanin, twenty-six. Left the hotel in the early hours of the morning. Bed not slept in, but an empty overnight bag left in her fourth-floor room. Forensics in there now.'

'What do the front desk say?' Eve asks.

'They say she's a looker. We're going through the CCTV footage.'

A dark certainty fills Eve. She feels beneath her Tyvek suit for her phone. Calls up the photograph of the woman at the meeting. 'Could that be her?'

The DCI stares at it. 'Where did you get this?'

Eve is telling him about the meeting when his phone rings, and he holds up a hand. Listens in frowning silence.

'OK,' he says. 'Turns out the credit card she showed the hotel when she checked in yesterday was stolen at Gatwick airport a week ago, from the real Julia Fanin. But we've got fingerprints and hopefully DNA from the overnight bag, and we're soon going to have some CCTV stills. Can you stick around?'

'For as long as it takes.' She glances at Simon. 'I'm afraid that shopping trip's going to have to wait.'

That afternoon Eve attends a meeting at Thames House, in the course of which she is questioned in detail as to her decision concerning Kedrin's protection and her subsequent change of mind, debriefed about the police inquiry, and finally, ordered to take ten days' home leave. That she will return to the office to discover she has been demoted or reassigned is a foregone conclusion.

At home, she can't settle. There are a hundred things to do about the flat – sorting, storing, cleaning, tidying – but

Eve can't bring herself to embark on any of them. Instead she goes for long, directionless walks through the snow on Hampstead Heath, constantly checking her phone. She's given Niko the bare bones of the situation and he doesn't press her for more, but she can tell that he's hurt and frustrated by his inability to help. She's always known that the secrecy aspect of intelligence work imposes its own unique strains on a marriage; what's shocking is just how corrosive it proves to be. How her silence eats away at the very foundations of the trust between herself and Niko.

The accommodation that they reached, early on in their marriage, was that while her working hours belonged to Thames House and the Service, at the end of the day she came home to him. What they shared – the complicity and intimacy of their evenings and nights – was infinitely more important than the things that they couldn't.

But the Kedrin murder spreads like a toxin into every aspect of her life. At night, instead of slipping into bed beside Niko and healing the rifts of the day by making love, she stays up until the early hours of the morning scanning the Internet, and hunting for new reports on the killings.

The Sunday papers make what they can of the case. The *Observer* hints at possible Mossad involvement, and the *Sunday Times* speculates that Kedrin might have been eliminated on the orders of the Kremlin because his increasingly fascist outpourings were beginning to embarrass the president. The police, however, release no more than the barest details. Certainly nothing about a female suspect. And then, on Wednesday morning, just as her toast is beginning to brown – Niko usually prepares breakfast, but he's already at work – Eve gets a call from DCI Hurst.

The DNA analysis on the hair samples found in the valise, a rush job by the forensic lab, has come up with a match on the UK database. An arrest has been made at Heathrow. Can Eve come to Paddington Green Police Station to assist with identification?

Eve can, and as she replaces the receiver, the smoke alarm goes off. Throwing the burning toast into the sink with a pair of salad tongs, she opens the kitchen window, and stabs vainly at the alarm with a broom-handle. I'm really not cut out for this domestic stuff, she thinks bleakly. Perhaps it's just as well I'm not pregnant. Not that that's exactly a likelihood, with the way things are going.

Paddington Green Police Station is a brutal, utilitarian building that smells of anxiety and stale air. Beneath ground level is a high-security custody suite where prisoners suspected of terrorist offences are held. The interview room is grey-painted and strip-lit; a one-way glass window takes up most of one wall. Eve and Hurst sit beneath it, with the prisoner sitting opposite them. It's the woman who was at Kedrin's lecture.

Eve is expecting to feel a fierce triumph at the sight of her. Instead, as at the Conway Hall, she's struck by her beauty. The woman, probably in her mid-twenties, has an oval, high-cheekboned face, framed by a dark, glossy bob. She's simply dressed in black jeans and a grey T-shirt that shows off her slender arms and neat, small-breasted frame. She looks tired, and more than a little confused, but no less graceful for all that, and Eve is suddenly conscious of her own shapeless hoodie and untended hair. What would I give to look like that? she wonders. My brain?

Hurst introduces himself and 'my colleague from the Home Office', and switching on the voice-recorder, officially cautions the suspect, who has elected to dispense with the services of a lawyer. And looking at her, Eve suddenly knows that something is wrong. That this woman is as incapable of murder as she is. That the police case is about to fall apart.

'Please state your name,' Hurst says to her.

The woman leans forward towards the voice-recorder. 'My name is Lucy Drake.'

'And your profession?'

She darts a look at Eve. Her eyes, even beneath the strip-lights, are a vivid emerald. 'I'm an actress. An actress and model.'

'And what were you doing at the Vernon Hotel in Red Lion Street, last Friday night?'

Lucy Drake gazes thoughtfully at her hands, which are folded on the table in front of her. 'Can I start at the beginning?'

Even as her heart sinks at how completely she and the police have been blindsided, Eve can't help but admire the elegance of the deception.

It all started, Lucy explains, with a call received by her agent. The client represented himself as belonging to a production company that was making a television series about different aspects of human behaviour. In this connection, they needed an attractive, confident young actress to undertake a series of social experiments, in which she would play a number of roles. The filming would take place over five days in London and Los Angeles, and the successful applicant would be paid four thousand pounds a day.

'It was all a bit vague,' Lucy says. 'But given the fee, and the exposure the programme would bring, I wasn't too worried. So that afternoon I took the tube from Queen's Park, where I live, to the St Martin's Lane Hotel, where they were holding the interviews. The director was there – Peter something, I think he was Eastern European – and a cameraman who was videoing everyone. There were several other girls there, and we were called in one by one.

'When it came to my turn Peter asked me to role-play a couple of scenes with him. One where I was booking into a hotel and I had to make the desk guy fall for me, and one where I had to approach a speaker after a lecture and seduce him, basically. The idea in both scenarios was to be super-flirty and charming but not come across like a hooker. Anyway, I gave it my best shot, and when I'd finished, he asked me to wait downstairs in this Cuban teahouse place and order anything I wanted. So I did, and forty minutes later he came down and said congratulations, I've seen everyone and the job's yours.'

Over the next two days 'Peter' went through everything that Lucy was required to do. She was measured for the clothes that she would wear, and told that this 'costume' had to be precisely adhered to, with no changes or substitutions. On Friday afternoon she was to book into the Vernon Hotel under the name of Julia Fanin and take an overnight bag up to her room. Peter would provide the credit card that she would use and also the bag, which she was not under any circumstances to open.

Leaving the bag in the room, she was to walk to the Conway Hall, around the corner in Red Lion Square, and buy a ticket to the 8 p.m. lecture given by Viktor Kedrin. After the lecture she was to gain personal access to Kedrin, charm and flatter him, and arrange to meet him at his hotel later that night. With that done, she was to meet Peter on the corner of the square, give him her hotel room key-card, and take a taxi home to Queen's Park.

The following morning, Lucy was told, Peter would pick her up early, drive her to Heathrow, and put her on a plane to Los Angeles. There she would be met, put up at a hotel, and given instructions for the second stage of filming.

'And that's how it worked out?' asks Hurst.

'Yes. He came round at 6 a.m. with a first-class return to LA, and I was in the air by nine. I was met at the airport by a driver who took me to the Chateau Marmont, where I got a message that the filming had been cancelled, but I was welcome to stay on at the hotel. So I used the time to go and see some acting agents, and at midday yesterday caught the return flight to Heathrow. Where I was, um . . . arrested. For murder. Which was kind of a surprise.'

'Really?' asks Hurst.

'Yes, really.' Lucy wrinkles her nose and looks around the interview room. 'You know, there's a really weird smell of burnt toast in here.'

An hour later, Eve and Hurst are standing on the steps at the rear of the police station, watching as an unmarked BMW turns out of the car park, headed for Queen's Park. Hurst is smoking. As the BMW passes, Eve catches a final glimpse of the flawless profile that she photographed in the Conway Hall.

'Do you think we're ever going to get a useful description of this Peter character?' Eve asks.

'Unlikely. We'll bring Lucy back to help us make up a Photofit when she's had a few hours' sleep, but I'm not hopeful. It was all far too well planned.'

'And you really don't think she was in on any of it?'

'No. I don't. We'll check her story out in detail, obviously, but my guess is that she isn't guilty of anything except naivety.'

Eve nods. 'She so much wanted it to be true. The successful audition, the big break into TV . . .'

'Yeah.' Hurst treads out his cigarette on the wet concrete step. 'He played her just right. And us, too.'

Eve frowns. 'So how do you think two of Lucy's hairs came to be in that overnight bag, if she never opened it?'

'My guess would be that Peter, or one of his people, took the hairs during the fake audition, perhaps out of her hairbrush. And then our shooter drops them in the bag after she's taken Lucy's place in the hotel. And here's a question for you. Why Los Angeles? Why go to the trouble of flying that girl halfway round the world when she's already played her part?'

'That's easy,' says Eve. 'To make sure she's out of the picture by the time the news of the murder breaks. They can't risk her reading about it online, or hearing about it on the radio, and going straight to the police with what she knows. So they make sure that she's taking off for LA – an eleven hour flight – at the precise time that the murder's discovered on Saturday morning. Which not only renders Lucy incommunicado, but also sets a perfect false trail, giving the real killer and her team plenty of time to cover their tracks and vanish.'

Hurst nods. 'And once she's at the swanky Sunset Boulevard hotel . . .'

'She's going to stay for the duration, exactly. She may, just possibly, see or read something about Kedrin, but that's all happening on the other side of the world. Meanwhile, she's got Hollywood agents to see. That's what's going to be uppermost in her mind.'

'And then, when they're ready, and the DNA results are in, they serve her up to us on a plate.' He shakes his head. 'You have to admire their cheek.'

'Yeah, well, cheeky or not, that woman shot four foreign nationals dead on our turf. Can we go back and see that CCTV footage again?'

'Absolutely.'

It's been edited into a single, silent loop. Lucy Drake walking into the hotel foyer in her parka, carrying the valise, and checking in, the suggestiveness of her body language apparent. Lucy exiting the lift on the fourth floor and walking to Room 416. Lucy leaving the hotel without the valise, raising the hood of her parka as she goes.

'OK stop,' Eve says. 'That's the last of her, agreed? From now on the woman in the parka is our killer.'

'Agreed,' says Hurst.

He runs the footage in x16 slow-motion. Infinitely slowly, as if moving through treacle, the hooded figure enters the hotel, lifts a blurry hand in the direction of the front desk, and vanishes out of shot. Her face is invisible, as it is throughout the footage in the hotel corridors.

'Look at her planting that bug outside Kedrin's room,' says Hurst. 'She knows she's on camera, but she doesn't care, she knows we can't make her. You have to admit, Eve, she's good.'

'You weren't able to pull any prints off the bug, or anywhere else?'

'Look closely. Surgical gloves.'

'Mother*fucker*,' Eve breathes.

Hurst raises an eyebrow.

'She's a murdering bitch, Gary, and she's cost me my job. I want her, dead or alive.'

'Good luck with that,' says Hurst.

At their Avenue Kléber apartment, Gilles Mercier and his wife Anne-Laure are entertaining. Among those at dinner are a junior minister from the Department of External Trade, the director of one of France's major hedge funds, and the executive vice president of Paris's most important fine art auction house. Given the company, Gilles has gone to considerable trouble to ensure that everything is just so. The food has been catered by Fouquet's on the Champs-Élysées, the wine (2005 Puligny-Montrachet, 1998 Haut-Brion) is from Gilles's own carefully curated cellar, and precisely dimmed spotlights pick out the cabinet of ormolu clocks and the two Boudin oils of the beach at Trouville, which the executive vice president has recognised as fakes, and indeed has whispered as much to his younger male companion.

The conversation among the men has covered predictable ground. Immigration, the fiscal naivety of the socialists, the Russian billionaires forcing up the price of holiday homes in Val-d'Isère and the Ile de Ré, and the upcoming season at the Opéra. Their wives and the executive vice president's friend, meanwhile, have covered the new Phoebe Philo collection, the fabulousness of Primark pyjamas, the latest Ryan Gosling film, and a charity ball that the hedge-fund director's wife is organising.

Invited by Anne-Laure to balance the numbers, Villanelle is bored senseless. The junior minister, whose knee has nudged hers more than once under the table, is questioning her about her activities as a day-trader, and she is answering in evasive generalities.

'So how was London?' he enquires. 'I was there in November. Were you very busy?'

'Yes, work's always murder. But it was lovely to be there. Hyde Park in the snow. The Christmas lights, the pretty shop windows . . .'

'And in the evenings?' He allows the question to hang suggestively in the air.

'In the evenings, I read and went to bed early.'

'Alone? In your Primark pyjamas?' This time it's his hand that finds her knee.

'Precisely. I'm afraid I'm a rather dull girl. Married to my work. But can I ask you, who does your wife's hair? That layered style looks lovely on her.'

The junior minister's smile grows fainter, and his hand moves away. The minutes tick by, glasses and plates are filled and refilled, Élysée Palace rumours and fifty-year-old Armagnac circulate. Finally the evening winds down and the guests are brought their coats.

'Come on,' says Anne-Laure, grabbing Villanelle by the arm. 'Let's go, too.'

'Are you sure?' murmurs Villanelle, eyeing Gilles, who is corking bottles and issuing instructions to the caterers.

'I'm sure,' hisses Anne-Laure. 'If I don't get out of this flat right now I'm going to scream. And look at you, all dressed up. If ever I saw a girl who needed an adventure . . .'

Five minutes later, the two of them are rounding the Arc de Triomphe at speed in Villanelle's silver Audi Roadster. It's a cold, clear night with tiny flecks of snow silvering the air. The Roadster's roof is lowered and Héloïse Letissier is blasting from the sound system.

'Where are we going?' Villanelle shouts, the icy wind whipping at her hair as they swing onto the Avenue des Champs-Élysées.

'Doesn't matter,' Anne-Laure mouths back. 'Just drive.'

Villanelle puts her foot down, and whooping and laughing, the two women race into the glittering darkness of the Paris night.

On the penultimate day of her enforced leave, an envelope bearing Eve's name falls through the letterbox of the flat. The writing paper is headed with the imprint of the Travellers Club, in Pall Mall. The unsigned message, handwritten in slanting italics, is short and to the point:

Please come to the office of BQ Optics Ltd. Second floor, above Goodge Street Underground Station tomorrow (Sunday) at 10.30 am. Bring this letter with you. Confidential.

Eve reads the note several times. The Travellers Club writing paper suggests that the correspondent has Security Services or Foreign Office connections, the fact that it is handwritten and hand-delivered suggests an entirely sensible distrust of email. It could of course be a hoax, but who would bother?

At 9.30 the next day she leaves Niko sitting at the kitchen table amid a sea of pamphlets. He's assessing the costs and benefits of converting the attic into a miniature hydroponic farm, sustained by low-energy LED lighting, and producing pak choi and broccoli.

The entrance to the BQ Optics office is on Tottenham Court Road. Noting it as she exits Goodge Street tube station, she crosses the road and watches the place for five minutes from outside Heal's, the furniture store. The tube station and the first-floor offices are faced with brown glazed tile, and surmounted by a dingy residential block. The second-floor offices appear deserted.

But when she presses the bell at the side of the entrance, she is buzzed in immediately. A staircase leads to the first floor, the headquarters of a recruitment agency, and thence by narrower stairs upwards. The door to the BQ Optics office is ajar. Feeling a little foolish, Eve pushes it open and stands back. Nothing happens for a moment, then a tall figure in an overcoat steps into the dusty light.

'Miss Polastri? Thank you for coming.'

'It's Mrs. And you are?'

'Richard Edwards, Mrs Polastri. My apologies.'

She recognises him, and is astounded. Former station chief in Moscow, now head of the Russia desk at MI6, he is a very senior figure indeed in the Intelligence world.

'And the cloak and dagger. Sorry for that, too.'

She shakes her head, bemused.

'Come in, take a seat.'

105

She walks through. The office is unheated and dusty, its windows almost opaque with grime. The only furniture is an elderly steel desk, with two takeaway cups of Costa coffee on it, and a pair of rust-scarred folding chairs.

'I guessed milk but no sugar.'

'Thank you, perfect.' She takes a sip.

'I've become aware of your situation at Thames House, Mrs Polastri.'

'Eve, please.'

He nods, his gaze austere in the dim light of the window.

'Let me save time. You are being held responsible for failing to prevent the murder of Viktor Kedrin at the hands of an unknown female. Your initial judgement was not to request Metropolitan Police protection for Kedrin, but you then changed your mind, and found this decision blocked. Correct?'

Eve nods. 'Substantially, yes.'

'My information, and you're going to have to take my word on this, is that this was not due to administrative inflexibility or departmental budget issues. Certain elements at Thames House, and indeed at Vauxhall Cross, were determined that Kedrin should be unprotected.'

She stares at him. 'You're saying that officers of the Security Services conspired to assist in his murder?'

'Something like that.'

'But . . . why?'

'The short answer is that I don't know. But there has definitely been pressure brought to bear. Whether this is an issue of ideology, corruption, or what the Russians call *kompromat* – essentially blackmail – it's impossible to say, but there's no shortage of individuals and institutions who would have liked to see Kedrin silenced. What he offered was the blueprint of a new, fascist superstate, implacably hostile to the capitalist West. It wouldn't have come into being tomorrow, but look a little further downstream, and the prospects are grim.'

'So you think those responsible might belong to some pro-Western, pro-democracy group?'

'Not necessarily. Could easily be another hard-right outfit, determined to do things their own way.' He stares at the traffic on Tottenham Court Road. 'I contacted the Russian foreign minister last week via . . . let's call it the old spies network. I promised him that as Kedrin was murdered on British soil, we would find his killer. He accepted this, but made it quite clear that until such time as we did so, a state of diplomatic hostility would exist between our respective nations.'

He turns to face her. 'Eve, I want you to go to Thames House tomorrow morning, and offer your resignation, which will be accepted. Then I want you to work for me. Not from Vauxhall Cross, but from this office, which we appear to own. You will receive an SIS executive grade salary, a deputy, and full tech-com support. Your mission, which you will prosecute by any means necessary, is to identify the killer of Victor Kedrin. You will discuss this with no one outside of your team, and you will answer only to me. Anything you need in the way of extra personnel – watcher teams, armed backup – you will clear through me, and only through me. In effect, you will operate as if in hostile territory. Moscow rules.'

Eve's thoughts are ricocheting all over the place. 'Why me?' she asks. 'Surely you've got—'

'To be brutal, because you're the one person that I know not to be compromised. How far the rot spreads, I can't say. But I've looked pretty closely at your record, and my judgement is that you're equal to the task.'

'Thank you.'

'Don't thank me. This is going to be hard and dangerous. Whoever this shooter is – and there are echoes of several high-profile international kills by a woman in the last couple of years – she's dug in deep, and she's very, very well protected. If you take this on, you must do the same thing. Dig in deep.' He looks around the bare, cold room. 'It's going to be a long winter.'

Eve stands there. She has the dizzying impression that the world has slowed. There's a moment of intense silence.

'I'll do it,' she says. 'I'll hunt her down. Whatever it takes.'

Richard Edwards nods. Holds out his hand. And Eve knows that nothing will ever be the same again.

3

It's almost seven in the evening when FatPanda leaves the rain-streaked building on Datong Road. June in Shanghai is a time of sweltering humidity and frequent downpours. The roads and pavements shine, cars and trucks hiss by in a shudder of exhaust, and the heat rises in waves from the wet tarmac. FatPanda is neither a young man nor a fit one, and his shirt is soon clinging sweatily to his back.

But it's been a good day. He and his White Dragon crew have launched a successful spear-phishing assault against a Belarusian company named Talachyn Aerospace, and have just begun the wholly satisfying business of draining the company's data, stealing passwords and project files, and generally making merry with its most sensitive information.

In the eight years of its existence, the White Dragon crew has hit the best part of a hundred and fifty military and corporate targets. Initially in the US, more recently in Russia and Belarus. Like most of its victims, Talachyn has offered only token resistance. A week ago, a junior employee received an email that purported to come from the company's director of security, inviting him to click on a link for information about a new firewall. In fact, the link contained the ZeroT downloader, a remote-access tool designed by FatPanda, giving his crew the run of Talachyn's operational files.

Since these relate to classified fighter-jet designs they will be of particular interest to FatPanda's superiors in Beijing. For the White Dragon group are not, as some have thought them, merely a gratuitously destructive team of hackers and anarchists. They are an elite cyber-warfare unit of the Chinese People's Liberation Army, engaged in targeted attacks on foreign corporations, military intelligence systems and infrastructure. The anonymous-looking building on Datong Road has been fitted out with banks of powerful computer servers and high-speed fibre-optic lines, all of them cooled by precision air-conditioning systems. FatPanda, the team's leader, is Lieutenant Colonel Zhang Lei, and it was he who chose the crew's title. A moon-white dragon, according to Chinese symbolism, embodies a ferocious supernatural power. It is an omen of death. A warning.

Ignoring the crowds of home-going workers and the clammy heat, FatPanda walks unhurriedly through the evening haze of the Pudong district, gazing around him with admiration at the city's trophy skyscrapers. At the soaring glass column of the Shanghai Tower, the silver-blue sliver of the World Financial Centre, and the vast, pagoda-like Jin Mao Tower. That things are rather less spectacular at street level, where beggars rummage through garbage-bins, is not of concern to FatPanda.

He is, in many ways, a clever and even brilliant man. He is certainly a lethal cyber-warrior. But success has led FatPanda to make a cardinal strategic error: he has under-estimated his enemy. While he and his crew have been rummaging through the intellectual property of foreign corporations, diverting terabytes of secret data to Beijing, the world's intelligence agencies and private security firms have not been idle. Their analysts have been amassing their own data: identifying Internet protocol addresses, reverse-engineering the White Dragon crew's malware, and following their actions keystroke by keystroke.

The information they've acquired, and the identities of FatPanda and his team, have been passed up the line. As yet, no Western or Russian administration has risked confrontation with Beijing by directly accusing the People's Liberation Army of state-sponsored data-theft; the diplomatic fallout would be too damaging. But others have been less concerned with such sensitivities. The predations of White Dragon have cost their victims billions of dollars over the years, and a group of individuals, collectively more powerful than any government, has decided that it is time to act.

A fortnight ago, at a meeting of the Twelve at a private seafront estate near Dartmouth, Massachusetts, Lieutenant Colonel Zhang Lei was the subject of a vote. All of the fish placed in the velvet drawstring bag were red.

Villanelle arrived in Shanghai a week ago.

FatPanda proceeds through the crowds and the diesel fumes of Pudong towards the Dongchang Road ferry terminal. He has been trained in the techniques of counter-surveillance, but it has been some years since he practised them with any real assiduity. He is on his own turf, and his enemies are continents away, little more than flickering usernames behind transparent passwords. That his actions could have deadly consequences has never seriously occurred to him.

Perhaps this is why, as he steps onto the ferry, he takes no notice of the young man in the business suit, just metres behind him, who has tailed him from his office, and who speaks briefly into his phone before vanishing into the hurrying throng on Dongchang Road. Or perhaps it's just that Lieutenant Colonel Zhang Lei's mind is elsewhere. For this prince of cyber-spies has a secret of his own, of which his colleagues know nothing. A secret which, as the ferry noses into the polluted currents of the Huangpu river, charges him with a dark thrill of anticipation.

He looks ahead of him, seeing and not seeing the illuminated panorama of the Bund, the kilometre-long waterfront on which stand the landmark edifices of old Shanghai. His gaze traverses the former banks and trading houses without interest. These monuments to colonial power are now luxury hotels, restaurants and clubs, the playground of rich tourists and the financial elite. His own destination lies beyond this gilded facade.

As he leaves the ferry at the South Bund terminal FatPanda performs a cursory sweep of his surroundings, but once again fails to register the operative reporting his progress, this time a young woman in the uniform of a hotel employee. Fifteen minutes later, he has left the Bund behind him, and is hurrying through the narrow, intersecting alleyways of the Old City. This district, teeming with shoppers and tourists, fragrant with moped exhaust and the fatty tang of street-food, is a far cry from the monumental splendour of the Bund. The pinched lanes are hung with laundry and loops of electrical cable, stalls attended by squatting women are piled high with rain-damp produce, tiny shops

112

behind bamboo-pole awnings sell fake antiques and retro-styled girly calendars. As FatPanda turns a corner a pimp on a scooter gestures towards a dimly lit interior in which rows of young prostitutes wait and whisper.

His pace urgent now, his heart pounding, FatPanda hurries past these temptations. His destination is a three-storey corner building on Dangfeng Road. At the entrance, he keys in a four-figure code. The door opens to reveal a middle-aged woman behind a reception desk. Something in the fixity of her smile suggests extensive maxillo-facial surgery.

'Mr Leung,' she says brightly, consulting her laptop. 'Please, go right on up.' He knows that she knows that Leung is not his name, but in the house on Dangfeng Road, a certain etiquette prevails.

The first floor is given over to more or less conventional sexual pleasures. As FatPanda climbs the stairs he is afforded a glimpse, through a briefly opening door, of a pink-lit room and a girl in a baby-doll nightie.

The second floor is altogether more specialist. FatPanda is met by an unsmiling young woman dressed in a crisp green and white skirted uniform. She wears a starched cap pinned to her upswept hair, a surgical mask, and a transparent plastic apron which rustles as she moves. She smells of some austere disinfectant. A name tag pinned to her chest identifies her as Nurse Wu.

'You're late,' she says icily.

'I'm sorry,' FatPanda whispers. He's already so excited that he's trembling.

Frowning, Nurse Wu leads him into a room dominated by a gurney, several monitors, and a ventilator. Beneath the ceiling light, an array of scalpels, retractors and other surgical instruments gleam dimly on aluminium trays.

'Remove your clothes and lie down,' she orders, indicating a pink hospital gown. The gown barely reaches FatPanda's fleshy hips, and as he takes his place on the gurney with his genitals exposed, he feels profoundly, thrillingly vulnerable.

Beginning with his arms, Nurse Wu begins to fasten a series of canvas and Velcro restraints, pulling the cuffs so tightly around FatPanda's chest, thighs and ankles that he is completely immobilised. The final restraint encircles his throat, and with the strap secured, she places a black rubber oxygen mask over his nose and mouth. His breathing is now audible as a shallow, urgent hissing.

'You understand that all this is for your own good?' says Nurse Wu. 'Some of the procedures you require are highly intrusive, and may be painful.'

FatPanda manages a faint groan from inside the mask. His panicked eyes skid around. For an instant, inches in front of his face, Nurse Wu's plastic apron falls forward and her gown parts to reveal a plump crotch in a pair of utilitarian, possibly military-issue, knickers.

'Now!' she says, and he hears the snap of latex gloves. 'You need a full bladder-flush. So I'm going to have to shave and catheterise you.'

FatPanda hears water running, feels the blood-temperature warmth as she lathers his pubic area and begins to scrape away with a surgical razor. Soon, his penis is rearing and twitching like a marionette. Laying down the razor, her eyes thoughtful above the three-ply surgical mask, Nurse Wu reaches for a pair of locking forceps from the tray. Holding them briefly in front of his face, she clamps the sharp teeth of the forceps onto the base of his scrotum. FatPanda looks up at her adoringly, tears of pain running down his cheeks. Once again, as if by the sheerest accident, he is permitted a glimpse of Nurse Wu's pillowy pudenda. He hears the clink of metal, feels the forceps lifted, and a moment later feels a fiery sensation tearing across his perineum.

'Now look at what you've made me do,' Nurse Wu murmurs exasperatedly, holding up a scalpel with a red-tinged blade. 'I'm going to have to stitch that.'

Tearing open a sterile pack, she takes out a monofilament suture line, and sets to work. The first entry of the needle makes FatPanda gasp, and as Nurse Wu wrenches the surgical knot tight, he shudders with barely containable pleasure. Frowning at this impertinence, Nurse Wu takes a chromium-plated probe from an ice-filled kidney dish, and inserts it forcibly into FatPanda's rectum. His eyes are closed now. He's in the zone, the place where terror and ecstasy meet in a dark, swirling tide.

And then suddenly, soundlessly, Nurse Wu is gone. FatPanda eyes drowsily revolve, scanning their limited field of vision, and another, different figure swims into view. Like Nurse Wu, she is dressed in surgical scrubs, cap, face-mask and gloves. But the eyes that are gazing at FatPanda are not amber brown like Nurse Wu's. They are the icy grey of the Russian midwinter.

FatPanda regards her with hazy surprise. A new practitioner is a departure from the scenario that he hasn't anticipated.

'I'm afraid things have got very serious,' she tells him, in English. 'That's why I've been called in.'

FatPanda's eyes shine with fearful anticipation. A *gweipo* surgeon. The clinic have excelled themselves.

Villanelle can tell from his expression that he understands what she has said. Not that she doubts for a moment that a man who has spent the best part of a decade reading the confidential files of international corporations is fluent in English. From a bag at her feet she takes an aluminium cylinder, just nine inches long. Disconnecting the airflow from the oxygen tank to FatPanda's rubber mask, she attaches it to the cylinder.

Pure carbon monoxide is odourless and tasteless. To the haemoglobin in the human body it is indistinguishable from oxygen. With the first cold rush of the gas into his nostrils, FatPanda feels the threads of reality drifting away. Twenty seconds later his breathing ceases.

When she's sure that he's dead, Villanelle reconnects the rubber mask to the oxygen. She has no doubt that someone with the specialist skills of Lieutenant Colonel Zhang Lei will receive a very thorough autopsy indeed, and that the true cause of his death will swiftly be revealed, but there's no harm in sowing a few seeds of confusion.

Kneeling, she examines the prostrate form of Nurse Wu. When Villanelle clamped a latex-gloved hand over her mouth, punched a hypodermic needle into her neck and injected a carefully measured dose of etorphine, the young Shanghainese woman managed a faint mew of surprise before slumping backwards into Villanelle's arms. Minutes later she still looks startled, but her breathing is steady; she will be conscious again in half an hour.

As an artistic touch, Villanelle slips off Nurse Wu's knickers and places them over FatPanda's head. Then, taking out a cheap mobile phone she has bought for cash that afternoon, she photographs him from a number of angles, none of them flattering. A final click emails the pictures, with a pre-written commentary, to half a dozen of China's most influential bloggers and dissidents. This is one story the Beijing establishment is not going to be able to cover up.

If there is a house rule common to the world's pleasure-houses, it is that the customer who is arriving must not meet the customer who is leaving. In the Dangfeng house a back stair leads to the exit, and it is this that Villanelle now takes, having changed from her surgical uniform. Outside, the streets are humid, and still teeming with tourists and strolling families, and no one takes any notice of a young Western woman wearing a baseball cap and carrying a small backpack. When pressed – and in the days and weeks to come there will be hard questions asked in the lanes and alleyways of the Old Town – one or two observers will recall that the woman's cap carried the insignia of the New York Yankees, and that her dark-blonde hair was worn in a ponytail, and from these slender impressions will be born the rumour that the suspect is an American. Frustratingly for the intelligence services and the police, no one will recall her face.

Ten minutes' walk is enough for Villanelle to dispose of the phone, battery and SIM card in separate restaurant garbage bins. The scrubs, gloves, mask and cap, together with the aluminium CO cylinder, sink to the murky bed of the Huangpu river in a string shopping bag weighted with stones.

*

Hours have passed, and Villanelle is lying in a claw-footed bathtub in a tenth floor apartment in Shanghai's exclusive French Concession, meditating upon the murder that she has just committed. The water is scented with essence of stephanotis, the walls are jade-green, silk curtains billow in the faint breeze.

As always on these occasions, the current of Villanelle's emotions ebbs and flows. There's satisfaction at a job well done. Detailed research, imaginative planning, and a clean, silent kill. Could anyone else have taken out FatPanda with such style, such frictionless ease? In her mind she replays his last moments. The surprise as their eyes met. Then that curious acceptance as he began the drift into the depths.

There's satisfaction, too, in the importance of her role. It's exhilarating to stand at the still centre of the turning world, and to know yourself an instrument of destiny. It makes up for the savage humiliations of her years as Oxana Vorontsova to know that she is not cursed, but blessed with a terrible strength.

Of all those humiliations, it's her rejection by the French teacher, Anna Ivanovna Leonova, that she still feels most keenly. A single woman in her late twenties, Leonova was more than a little awed by her troubled pupil's precocious linguistic gifts, and ignoring Oxana's rudeness and grace-lessness, determined to open her eyes to a world beyond the grey confines of Perm. So there were weekend sessions in Anna's tiny apartment, discussing Colette and Françoise Sagan, and on one memorable occasion a visit to the Tchaikovsky Theatre, to see a performance of the opera *Manon Lescaut*.

Oxana was bemused by the attention. No one had ever expended so much time on her. What Anna Ivanovna was giving her, she realised, was something selfless, something close to love. Intellectually, Oxana understood such an emotion, but she also knew herself incapable of feeling it. Physical desire, though, was another matter, and she lay awake, night after night, tortured by a raw longing for her teacher that she could find no way of expressing beyond a sullen blankness.

Not that the teenage Oxana was a novice when it came to sex. She had tried both men and women, and found no difficulty in manipulating both. But with Anna she dreamt of a realm of the senses that lay beyond the beery fumblings of bikers behind the Bar Molotov, or the rough tongue of the female security guard at the TsUM department store who had caught her stealing, marched her to the toilets, and buried her face between Oxana's thighs as the price of silence.

She tried, just once, to take things further with Anna. It was the evening they went to *Manon Lescaut*. They were sitting in the balcony, in the back row of seats, and towards the end of the opera Oxana had inclined her head against the teacher's shoulder. When Anna responded by putting an arm around her, Oxana was so overwhelmed she could hardly breathe.

As Puccini's music swirled around them, Oxana reached out a hand and laid it over one of Anna's breasts. Gently, but firmly, Anna removed the hand, and equally firmly, a moment later, Oxana replaced it. This was a game she had played many times in her mind.

'Stop it,' Anna said quietly.

'Don't you like me?' Oxana whispered.

The teacher sighed. 'Oxana, of course I do. But that doesn't mean . . .'

'What?' She parted her lips, her eyes searching for Anna's in the half dark.

'It doesn't mean . . . *that.*'

'Then fuck you, and fuck your stupid opera,' Oxana hissed, rage rising uncontainably inside her. Standing, she stumbled towards the exit, and ran down the staircase to the street. Outside, the city was lit by the sulphurous glow of night, and flurries of snow whirled in the car headlights on Kommunisticheskaya Prospekt. It was freezing cold, and Oxana realised that she had left her jacket inside the theatre.

She was too furious to care. Why didn't Anna Ivanovna want her? That culture stuff was all very well, but she needed more from Anna than that. She needed to see desire in her eyes. To see everything that gave her power over Oxana – her gentleness, her patience, her fucking *virtue* – dissolve into sexual surrender.

But Anna resisted this transformation. Even though, deep down she felt exactly the same way, and Oxana knew this to be true, because she had felt the flutter of the other woman's heart beneath her hand. It was intolerable, unbearable. And there in the theatre doorway, one hand thrust down the front of her jeans, Oxana gasped out her frustration until she sank to her knees on the icy pavement.

Anna forgave her for her behaviour at the Tchaikovsky Theatre, but Oxana never quite forgave Anna, and her feelings for her teacher took on a morbid, angry cast.

When Anna was sexually assaulted, matters reached a

head. Taking her father's combat knife, Oxana lured Roman Nikonov into the woods, and put things right. Nikonov survived, which wasn't part of her plan, but otherwise things went perfectly.

Oxana was never questioned, and if she'd have preferred her victim to die of shock and blood loss, at least she had the satisfaction of knowing that he'd be pissing through a tube for the rest of his life. She'd said as much to Anna Leonova, laying the story at her teacher's feet like a cat bringing home a mutilated bird.

With Anna's reaction, Oxana's world collapsed. She'd hoped for gratitude, admiration, profuse thanks. Instead the teacher had stared at her in icy, horrified silence. Only her knowledge of the conditions that Oxana would face in a women's penitentiary, Anna said, prevented her from contacting the police immediately. She would remain silent, but she never wished to see or speak to Oxana again.

The injustice of it, and the lacerating sense of loss, brought Oxana to the brink of suicide. She considered taking her father's Makarov pistol, going round to Anna's place, and shooting herself. Showering the little flat on Komsomolsky Prospekt with her blood and brains. Perhaps she'd have sex with Anna first; a 9mm automatic was a pretty persuasive seduction accessory.

In the end, though, Oxana did nothing. And the part of her that had yearned so desperately to make Anna her own simply froze.

Lying in the scented water in the Shanghai apartment, Villanelle feels her earlier elation displaced by an undertow of melancholy. She turns her head towards the window, a sweep of plate glass framing the glimmering dusk and the rooftops of the French Concession, and bites pensively at her upper lip. In front of the window is a Lalique bowl of white peonies, their petals soft and enfolding.

She knows that she should lie low. That to go out on the prowl for sex, tonight of all nights, would be reckless. But she also recognises the hunger inside herself. A hunger whose grip will only tighten. Stepping from the bath, wreathed in steam, she stands naked in front of the plate glass, and considers the infinity of possibilities before her.

It's after midnight when she walks into the Aquarium. The club is in the basement of a former private bank on the North Bund, and entrance is by personal introduction only. Villanelle was told about the Aquarium by the wife of a Japanese property developer whom she met at the Peninsula Spa in Huangpu. A stylish, gossipy woman, Mrs Nakamura explained to Villanelle that she usually went there on Friday nights. 'And alone, rather than in the company of my husband,' she added, with a meaningful sideways glance.

Certainly the name Mikki Nakamura is one the doorman knows. He shows Villanelle through an interior door to a spiral staircase winding down to a spacious, dim-lit subterranean chamber. The place is crowded, and an animated buzz of conversation overlays the muted pulse of the music.

For a moment Villanelle stands at the foot of the stairs, looking around her. The most striking feature is a floor-to-ceiling wall of glass, perhaps ten metres long. A moving shadow darkens its luminous blue expanse, and then another, and Villanelle realises that she is looking into a shark tank. Hammerheads and reef sharks glide past, the underwater lights painting their skins with a satin sheen.

Mesmerised, Villanelle makes her way towards the tank. The smell of the club is that of wealth, a heady mix of frangipani blossom, incense and designer-scented bodies. In the tank a tiger shark drifts into view, and fixes Villanelle with its blank, indifferent gaze.

'Dead eyes,' says Mikki Nakamura, materialising beside her. 'I know too many men who look like that.'

'We all do,' says Villanelle. 'And women, too.'

Mikki smiles. 'I'm glad you came,' she murmurs, running a finger down Villanelle's black silk qipao dress. 'This is Vivienne Tam, isn't it? It's lovely.'

Villanelle mirrors Mikki's smile and compliments her on her own outfit. At the same time, she's running a security check, scanning the club for anything or anyone out of place. For the nondescript figure in the shadows. The eyes that look away too quickly. The face that doesn't fit.

Her attention is snagged by a willowy figure in a white halter-top and miniskirt. Mikki follows Villanelle's gaze and sighs. 'Yes, I know what you're thinking. Who let the dogs out?'

'Pretty girl,' says Villanelle.

'Girl? Up to a point. That's Janie Chou, one of Alice Mao's ladyboys.'

'Who's Alice Mao?'

'She owns this club. In fact she owns this building. She's one of the richest women in Shanghai, thanks to the sex-trade.'

'Obviously quite a businesswoman.'

'That's one way of putting it. She's certainly not the sort of person you want to get on the wrong side of. But let me get you a drink. The watermelon Martinis are fabulous.'

'And fabulously strong, I bet.'

'Relax, sweetie,' says Mikki. 'Have *fun*.'

As the other woman joins the crush at the small art deco bar, behind which an elegant young person is shaking cocktails, Villanelle allows herself to be swept along by a gesticulating crowd of young Chinese men, all designer-dressed to within an inch of their lives.

'I don't think you have what they want,' says a soft voice at her side. 'But I might have what *you* want.'

Villanelle looks into the pretty, upturned eyes of Janie Chou. 'And what's that?'

'Full girlfriend experience? Kissing on the mouth, lots of nice sucking and fucking, then afterwards I cook for you?'

'Perhaps not tonight. I've had a killing day.'

Janie leans in close, so that Villanelle can smell the jasmine flowers in her hair. 'I got crabs,' she whispers.

Villanelle raises an eyebrow.

'No, silly! In my fridge, not my lady-garden! Hairy crabs. Very expensive.'

Mikki approaches with two brimming Martini glasses and hands one to Villanelle, pointedly ignoring Janie. 'Someone I want you to meet,' she says, taking Villanelle's arm and steering her away.

'What are hairy crabs?'

'A local delicacy,' says Mikki. 'Unlike that little prostitute.'

She introduces Villanelle to a handsome young Malaysian man in a seersucker suit. 'This is Howard,' she says, clearly anxious for Villanelle's approval. 'Howard, meet Astrid.'

They shake hands, and Villanelle summons the details of her cover story. Astrid Fécamp, twenty-seven-year-old columnist for *Bilan21*, a French-language investment newsletter. Like all her legends, this one has been very carefully constructed. Should anyone care to investigate Mademoiselle Fécamp online, they will discover that she has been a contributing editor of *Bilan21* for two years, and specialises in petrochemical futures.

But Howard is too busy lavishing compliments on Mikki to concern himself with such minutiae. 'Fuchsia!' he breathes, standing back to admire her Hervé Léger cocktail dress. 'The perfect colour for you.'

Privately, Villanelle thinks the colour a disaster. Against her pale ivory complexion it makes Mikki look like Howard's mother. But perhaps that's what Howard likes.

'So what do you do?' Villanelle asks. 'Are you in the fashion business?'

'Not as such. I have a concept spa in Xintiandi.'

'It's heaven,' Mikki breathes. 'There's a rock garden and an Evian ice fountain and Buddhist monks to align your chakras and do your hair.'

'Sounds fabulous. I'm sure my chakras are all shot to fuck.'

'Well then.' Howard smiles. 'You must come visit.'

As soon as she can decently extract herself, Villanelle leaves them alone. Circulating, Martini glass in hand, she soon finds herself face to face with the sharks again. And, moments later, with Janie Chou.

'Come with me,' Janie says, her features soft in the lunar glow of the tank. 'Someone wanna meet you.'

'Who?'

'Come.' Her slim hand takes Villanelle's.

In a dim-lit alcove, a woman is sitting alone, scrolling through the messages on her phone. She's Eurasian, and when she looks up to dismiss Janie with a casual sweep of one hand, Villanelle sees that she has eyes of the palest glass-green.

'Janie's right,' says the woman. 'You're beautiful. Won't you sit down?'

Villanelle inclines her head in acceptance. From the woman's proprietorial manner she guesses that this is Alice Mao.

'So. Do you like my club?'

'It's . . . fun. Things could happen here.'

'Trust me, things do.' Amusement touches the glass-green eyes. 'Will you have some tea? One of those Martinis is quite enough, in my experience.'

'That would be nice. My name is Astrid, by the way.'

'It suits you. Mine, as you know, is Alice. What is your occupation, Astrid?'

'Financial forecasting. I write for an investors' newsletter.'

Alice Mao frowns. 'Do you now?'

'Yes.' Villanelle holds her gaze. 'I do.'

'I've met a lot of finance people in my time, Astrid, and none of them is remotely like you.'

'So what am I like?'

'On the basis of our brief acquaintance, I'd say you're rather like me.'

Villanelle smiles, allowing Alice's cool regard to flood her veins. Something in the other woman's features, the way the taut line of her cheekbone softens into the curve of her chin, stirs her. She knows that such feelings are dangerous, but there are times when the secrecy and the almost feral caution with which she has to conduct her life become unbearable.

Alice glances at her phone. She stands, her midnight-blue dress rippling with the same underwater gleam as the sharks. 'Follow me.'

She leads Villanelle to a door, and a lift. The noise and the music die, there's a dizzying ascent, and Villanelle follows Alice into a rooftop apartment as dimly lit as the club. There's a folding gold-leaf screen, and shadowy contemporary paintings on the walls, but the room is dominated by a dramatic expanse of plate-glass window. Far below them is the city, its sprawling glitter made vague by a shroud of smog.

'The whore of Asia. That's what they used to call Shanghai. And it's still true. This apartment, the club, this building . . . All paid for by sex. Tea?' She indicates a spotlit side table. 'It's Silver Needle from Fuding Province. I think you'll like it.'

Villanelle sips the pale infusion. It tastes of fragrant, rainswept hillsides.

'I could make you very rich,' says Alice. 'I have clients who would pay a great deal of money for a night with you.'

Villanelle looks out into the night. She can smell the other woman's scent, and her hair. 'And you, Alice. What would you pay for me? Right here and now?'

Alice looks at her, her smile unwavering. 'Fifty thousand *kuai*.'

'A hundred thousand,' says Villanelle.

Alice tilts her head thoughtfully, then steps round to face Villanelle. Green eyes meet grey. 'For a hundred thousand *kuai*,' she says, undoing the silk-covered button at Villanelle's collar, 'I would expect a lot.'

Villanelle nods, and stands there, unmoving, as Alice's fingers move down her qipao dress. She closes her eyes, feels the silk lifted from her shoulders, and her underwear removed. Naked, she feels the floor tilt beneath her feet. She tries to speak Alice's name but it comes out as Anna, and when she tries to whisper 'fuck me', what she actually says is 'kill me'.

Four days later Eve Polastri and Simon Mortimer step from the air-conditioned cool of the Pudong airport arrivals building into the 30-degree heat of the taxi rank. It's midnight. Exhaust-tainted humidity rolls over them like a wave. Eve feels her scalp moisten and her H&M cotton twinset wilt on her shoulders.

Standing there in the taxi queue, her suitcase at her side, Eve knows that she's not the sort of woman who gets noticed. Since landing an hour earlier the only person who's given her a second glance is the Chinese customs officer who checked her passport, perhaps struck by the quiet intensity of her gaze. Both she and Simon look older than their years. Their fellow British Airways travellers, if they've given the matter any thought at all, have assumed that they are a married couple.

Simon glances at her affectionately. She reminds him of a starling or a thrush, one of those birds that patrol the lawn with sharp eyes and stabbing beaks. The hunter-killers of the intelligence world, like those of the animal kingdom, often have drab plumage.

Eve finds her own appearance mystifying. 'Do you think I could be pretty?' she asked her mother, shortly before going up to Cambridge to read Criminology and Forensic Psychology.

'I think you're very clever,' her mother replied.

It took her husband, Niko, a Polish-born maths teacher, to tell Eve that she was beautiful. 'Your eyes are like the Baltic Sea,' he said, drawing a finger down her transparently pale cheek. 'The colour of petrol.'

'You're such a bullshitter.'

'Only when I want sex.'

'A bullshitter *and* a pervert.'

He shrugged. 'I didn't marry you for your cooking.'

She misses him already.

Flagging down a taxi, a green Volkswagen Santana, Simon gives the driver the address of their hotel.

'I didn't know you spoke Mandarin,' Eve says.

Simon runs a hand over his stubble-roughened jaw. 'I did a year of it at university. If this guy starts a real conversation, I'm stuffed.'

'So does he know where the Sea Bird Hotel is?'

'I think so. His expression suggested he didn't think much of it.'

'Let's see. Discreet was how Richard Edwards described it.'

Eve and Simon's visit is strictly non-official, so there's no one from the Shanghai MI6 station to meet them. Indeed, everything about their status is irregular. Since her recruitment by Edwards to investigate the Kedrin killing, an operation run strictly off-the-books, Eve has not contacted a single one of her former colleagues. Instead, day after day, week after week, she has made her way to the cramped and dingy office over Goodge Street tube station. There, with the long-suffering Simon, she has scrolled through file after classified file, staring at her computer screen until her head pounds and her eyes ache with tiredness, in the search for anything – a whisper, an afterthought, the ghost of a suggestion – that might lead her closer to the woman who murdered Viktor Kedrin.

And she's got nowhere. She's identified several high-profile political and criminal killings in which a woman is rumoured to have been involved, and a handful which she's almost certain were carried out by a female shooter. She has watched, more times than she can remember, the CCTV recording from Kedrin's London hotel in which his killer can be seen coming and going. But the images are smeared and indistinct, even when fully enhanced, and the figure's face is never visible.

When not scouring cyberspace, Eve has followed the real-world lines of inquiry presented by the Kedrin case. But every lead, no matter how initially promising, has brought her up against a smoothly impermeable barrier. There's no witness, no forensic evidence, no useful ballistics, no money or paper trail. At a certain point, everything just cuts out.

Despite this lack of progress, Eve has a sense of the woman she's hunting. The woman she sometimes calls *Chernaya Roza* – Black Rose – after the 9mm Russian hollowpoint ammunition used to kill Kedrin and his bodyguards. Eve thinks that her Black Rose is in her mid-twenties, highly intelligent, and a loner. She is audacious, cool under pressure, and supremely skilled at compartmentalising her emotions. In all probability she is a sociopath, wholly lacking in affect and conscience. She will have few or no friends, and such relationships as she forms will be over-whelmingly manipulative and sexual in nature. Killing, in all probability, will have become necessary to her, with each successful murder further proof of her untouchability.

It's less than twenty-four hours since Richard Edwards walked unannounced into the office over the tube station.

'Does anyone ever clean this place?' he enquired, with vague distaste.

'Yes, Simon does. And very occasionally me. Sorry if it's not up to Vauxhall Cross standards. We've ordered some more vacuum cleaner bags.'

'Well, that's something to look forward to. And in the meantime . . .' He opened the briefcase at his feet, and took out two well-used passports and a sheaf of flight tickets and schedules. 'You're going to China. Tonight. Someone's taken out the leader of their cyber-warfare team in Shanghai, and it's thought that the hit was carried out by a woman.'

It took him less than five minutes to bring her up to speed on the demise of Lieutenant Colonel Zhang Lei. 'Your brief,' he told her, 'is to make discreet contact with the MSS, the Chinese Ministry of State Security, and convey my assurances that the murder of Zhang was not spon-sored, enabled or executed by us. Furthermore, you are to offer them any assistance they might need in investigating the murder, including sharing our suspicions about a female contract killer.'

'Do I have a contact at the MSS?'

'Yes. His name is Jin Qiang. I knew him in Moscow, when he was their head of station there, and he's a good man. Since then he and I have kept certain back-door channels open. He knows you're coming.'

'Isn't he going to wonder why he's dealing with me, rather than one of the local station officers? Who are presumably already on the case.'

'He'll guess there are sensitivities. Reasons why you can't go in under official cover.'

'So do we make contact with the MI6 station at all?'

Edwards stood, walked to the window, and peered through the grime at the traffic. 'For safety's sake, we have to assume that the conspiracy to cover this woman's tracks has global reach. If she's killing people in Shanghai, they'll have people there. Possibly our people. So you've got to keep clear of them. We can't afford to trust anyone.'

'How much can I tell the MSS guy?'

'Jin Qiang? As far as our hitwoman goes, you've got nothing to lose by giving him everything you've got.' He drained his coffee, and dropped the paper cup into the bin. 'We need to catch her, he needs to catch her.'

The door swung open. 'You know, I'm convinced Goodge Street station's a portal to hell,' said Simon, shrugging his computer bag from his shoulders onto his desk. 'I've just had such a Buffy moment . . .' He froze. 'Oh, hello, Richard.'

'Hello, Simon. Good morning.'

'We're going to Shanghai,' said Eve, and wondered what on earth she was going to tell Niko.

'Look at this,' Simon says, lowering the window of the taxi and flooding it with the warm night. 'It's extraordinary.'

And it is. They're approaching the Nanpu Bridge, with vast office blocks to right and left of them, their numberless windows pinpricks of gold against the bruised purple of the sky. And suddenly Eve's tiredness evaporates, and she's light-headed with the novelty of it all. Everything's about money and profit. You can see it in the soaring high-rises, smell it in the diesel fumes, taste it on the night air. The hunger. The high stakes and the huge returns. The unbridled sense that more is more.

It's an impression that's confirmed as they cross the bridge. Below them, boats festooned with tiny lights ply the dark expanse of the river. To their right, in floodlit splendour, waits the Bund.

'How d'you feel?' Eve asks him.

He leans forward, his buff linen jacket folded on his lap. 'I'm not sure. Things have got very strange recently.'

'She's out there,' Eve murmurs. 'Our Black Rose.'

'We don't know for certain that it was her who killed the hacker.'

'Oh, it was her all right.'

'Assuming it was. Why would she stick around?'

'Can't you guess?'

'No. To be honest with you, I can't.'

'For me, Simon. She's waiting for me.'

'Now you're actually starting to sound mad. I'm putting it down to jet lag.'

'You wait.'

He closes his eyes. Five minutes later they're at the hotel.

It's only when she's in her room, a functional space whose off-white walls are decorated with a single out-of-date calendar, that she allows herself to think about Niko. The phone call after Edwards left the office was horrible. It would have been easy enough to think up a cover story, but she couldn't bring herself to lie, and told Niko simply that she had to go away for a few days. He listened, said 'I see', and hung up. He has no idea where she is, or when she will be coming home. Eve stares out of the window. There's a road, and beyond it the dark gleam of water. A cluster of houseboats, showing dim lights.

She loves Niko, and she's hurting him deeply, and this is especially agonising because, for all his wisdom and experience, she can't help thinking of herself as his protector. She's guarding him from the truth about herself. From the side of her that he knows exists, but that he chooses not to acknowledge. The side of her that is utterly absorbed by the woman she is hunting, and the dark, refracted world in which she exists.

'They're staying at the Sea Bird Hotel on Suzhou Creek,' says Konstantin. 'They got in last night.'

Villanelle nods. The two of them are sitting in the tenth-floor apartment in the French Concession. On the table between them is a bottle of Tibet Glacier mineral water, two glasses, and a packet of Kosmos cigarettes.

'Which means that they're not here officially,' Konstantin continues. 'The Sea Bird is dirt cheap, by Shanghai standards.'

Villanelle stares out at the pale glare of the sky. 'So why do you think they've come?'

'We both know why they've come. The Polastri woman was asking questions in London after Kedrin's death, as I told you at the time. If she's here, it's because she's made the right connections.'

'Which means that she's smart. Or lucky. And that I need to get a close look at her.'

'No. That would be reckless. I'm pretty sure Polastri's got no real clue what's going on, but that doesn't mean she's not dangerous. Leave her to me, and go back to Paris. We need to wind this operation up. The hacker's dead, and you need to disappear.'

'I can't do that.'

His expression hardens. 'This is not how I want things to be between us, Villanelle. I don't want to have to negotiate every decision.'

'I know you don't. You want me to be your killer doll. Wind me up, point me at the target, *bang bang* and back in my box.' She looks him in the eye. 'Sorry, but that's not how I function these days.'

'I see. So how do you function, exactly?'

'Like a thinking, feeling human being.'

He looks away. 'Please, Villanelle, don't talk to me about feelings. You're better than that. *We're* better than that.'

'Are we?'

'Yes. We see the world for what it is. A place where there's only one law: survival. You survive very comfortably, do you not?'

'Maybe.'

'And why's that? Because give or take a couple of reckless incidents, you've obeyed the rules. What did I tell you in London?'

She looks away irritably. 'That I'm never completely safe. And that I should never fully trust anyone.'

'Exactly. Remember that, and you're fine. Forget it and you're fucked.' He reaches for the cigarettes. 'Forget it and we're all fucked.'

Frowning, Villanelle walks to the plate-glass door to the balcony and pulls it open. Humid air fills the room.

'Worried about your health?' Konstantin asks, lighting a Kosmos. 'I'd have thought a bullet in the back of the head was a more pressing concern.'

She looks at him. The acrid tobacco smell reminds her of their earliest days together. In Russia, he must have smoked at least a packet a day. 'So who's going to shoot me? Eve Polastri? I don't think so.'

'Trust me, Villanelle, her people will kill you without a second thought. One word from Polastri to Edwards, and MI6 will send in an E Squadron action team. Which is why you have to get out, *now*. Shanghai's a big place if you're Han Chinese, but it's a very small town if you're not. You could run into her anywhere.'

'I won't, don't worry. But I do have a way of getting to her. And perhaps of finding out what she knows.'

'Really?' He exhales cigarette smoke, which drifts away on the warm breeze. 'And would you kindly tell me how?'

She does so, and for a long time he's silent. 'It's too dangerous,' he says eventually. 'Too many variables. We could end up attracting exactly the wrong kind of attention.'

'You once told me that kind of operation was a speciality of yours.' She looks at him speculatively. 'Fear, sex and money, you said. The three great persuaders.'

'It's too dangerous,' he repeats.

She looks away. 'We might never get this chance again. We can't afford not to take it.'

He stands up. Walks out onto the balcony. Finishes his cigarette, taking his time, and flicks the end out into space.

136

'If we do it,' he says. 'You stay out of sight. I make the play. Agreed?'

She grins, her expression fierce.

'Shit,' says Eve, staring at her phone. 'That's a bad start.'

'Tell me,' says Simon.

She sits down on her unmade hotel bed. The room is small, with worn bamboo furniture and a distant view of the creek. Underwear is visible in Eve's open suitcase, and she wishes they'd agreed to meet downstairs.

'It's Hurst.' She hands him the phone. 'The Fanin credit card trail's gone dead.'

DCI Gary Hurst is the senior investigating officer on the Viktor Kedrin case. He has been following up a loose end which, just conceivably, could indicate an error on the part of those who set up Kedrin's murder. It seems that the theft of the card used by Lucy Drake to check into the hotel was reported to the police by Julia Fanin, but not to her bank. As a consequence, the hotel registration went through unchecked.

This discrepancy puzzled Hurst, especially when Fanin insisted that she had rung her bank's Lost and Stolen Card number, a claim validated by her mobile phone records. It turns out that the bank's credit-card support services are outsourced to a call-centre company based near Swindon, in the south-west of England, and Hurst's investigation has concluded that one of the company's employees unfroze the card after it was reported missing, so that it remained usable. Thousands of pounds worth of clothes, flights and hotel bills were then charged to the account over a two-week period, at the end of which the expenditure stopped dead. Which is where the investigation has stalled. Hurst's text reads:

> *Right now working thru 90+ employees who might have taken JF's call. But relevant records deleted so not confident of a result.*

'And even if by some miracle he gets a result, it's a dead cert we'd just hit another cut-out,' says Simon, returning Eve's phone.

She slips it into her bag. 'Let's go and see Jin Qiang. The taxi should be waiting downstairs.'

Opened in 2009, the first new building on the Bund for seventy years, the Peninsula Hotel is dauntingly grand. The lobby is pillared art deco, a tone-poem in ivory and old gold. The carpets are vast, the conversation muted. White-uniformed bellboys hurry discreetly between the vast reception desk and the near-silent lifts.

In the online catalogue, Eve's mint-green shift dress was described as a 'chic, summery office staple', but catching sight of herself in a mirror in the lift, she senses that she's striking the wrong note. The dress is sleeveless and she's cut herself shaving – her armpit still stings quite badly – so somehow she has to conduct a vital meeting with a senior officer of the Chinese Ministry of State Security without ever raising her right arm.

Jin Qiang is alone in the suite. It's vast, soft-lit and restfully luxurious. Sky-blue curtains frame a view of the river, and more distantly the skyscrapers of Pudong.

'Mrs Polastri, Mr Mortimer. This is a great pleasure.'

'Thank you for agreeing to see us,' says Eve, as she and Simon lower themselves into silk-upholstered armchairs.

'I have most affectionate memories of Richard Edwards. I trust he's in good health?'

For some minutes, the niceties are observed on both sides. Jin is a quietly spoken figure in a dove-grey suit. He speaks English with a faint American accent. At intervals a look of refined melancholy touches his features, as if he's saddened by the vagaries of human behaviour.

'The murder of Zhang Lei,' Eve begins.

'Yes, indeed.' He steeples his long, manicured fingers.

'We wish to convey our assurances that this action was not sponsored, executed or in any way enabled by agents of the British government,' Eve says. 'We have had our differences with your ministry, particularly concerning the activities of the individuals calling themselves the White Dragon. A unit, we have reason to believe, of the Chinese military. But this is not the way we would choose to resolve those differences.'

Jin smiles. 'Mrs Polastri, you are mistaken in thinking that the White Dragon group is part of the Chinese People's Liberation Army. They, and others like them, are just mischief-makers, acting without reference to anyone.'

Eve inclines her head diplomatically. This, she knows, is the official line on all cyber-attacks originating in China.

'We're here in Shanghai to assist in any way we can,' says Simon. 'Especially with reference to the killer of Lieutenant Colonel Zhang.'

'He was, I'm afraid, just plain Mr Zhang.'

'Of course. My apologies. But we understand that Richard Edwards has communicated to you our suspicions concerning a female assassin?'

139

'He has. And I'm aware of the circumstances surrounding the death of Viktor Kedrin.'

Eve leans forward in her chair. 'Let me cut to the chase. We believe that the woman who killed Kedrin also killed Zhang Lei. We believe she is not acting alone, but on behalf of an organisation of considerable reach and power.'

'That is indeed cutting to the chase, Mrs Polastri. May I ask what Zhang Lei and Viktor Kedrin had in common, that they should both be ... *eliminated* by this organisation?'

'At this stage it's hard to say. But I would repeat that neither we nor our American colleagues had any hand in the death of Zhang Lei. Nor that of Viktor Kedrin.'

Jin folds his hands in his lap. 'I must accept your assurances.'

Eve is suddenly conscious of the cut under her arm. For a ghastly moment she wonders if she has left a bloodstain on the silk upholstery of her chair. 'May I be frank with you?' she asks.

'Please do.'

'Richard Edwards's belief, which we share, is that a covert organisation – as yet unidentified – is committing these murders. We don't know their purpose or agenda. We don't know who they are, or how many. But we suspect that they have people placed in our own organisation and also in MI5, for whom I used to work. And almost certainly in other intelligence services.'

Jin frowns. 'I'm not sure how I can help you.'

Eve feels the meeting slipping from her grasp. 'Our only way forward, as things stand, is to follow the money. Is there anyone in the Western security services, Mr Jin, whom

140

you know or suspect to be in the pay of an organisation such as I have described?'

Silence swirls dizzyingly around her. She senses Simon's shock at the impropriety of her question.

Jin's features remain impassive. 'Perhaps we might order some tea,' he suggests.

'Have you seen my black cardigan?' Villanelle asks. 'The Annabel Lee one, with the pearl buttons?'

In answer, Alice Mao groans. She's lying on her bed opposite a young man with chiselled features and a gym-toned body which gleams like oiled teak. Both of them are naked. Beneath the silk sheet, the man's hand is moving rhythmically between Alice's legs. It's half past two in the afternoon.

'I'm sure I left it here somewhere,' Villanelle murmurs.

Exasperated, Alice rolls onto her stomach. 'Please. Just come to bed?'

'I have to go shopping.'

'Now?'

Villanelle shrugs.

'Ken's very much in demand, you know,' Alice says. 'He's doing us a huge favour, fitting us in like this.'

Villanelle knows Ken's story, because Alice has told it to her. How he was a student at Hong Kong University, completing an MA dissertation on the late poetry of Sylvia Plath, when he was talent-spotted in a hotel steam room. How he became Ken Hung, the most famous porn star in China.

As if on cue, Ken throws back the sheets. 'Ladies, we have wood!'

Alice gasps. 'Oh my goodness, it's just like in the films. Bigger, even. Sweetie, at least have a little stroke.'

'Sorry, but I really don't want that thing anywhere near me. I just want my black cardigan.' Villanelle frowns. 'You don't happen to know somewhere I can buy nice kitchen stuff, do you?'

'You could try Putua Parlour on Changhua Lu,' says Ken, complacently regarding the most famous penis in China. 'I get all my bakeware there. I'm a *big* Nigella fan.'

An hour later, Villanelle is strolling down one of the many aisles of Putua Parlour, noting the positioning of the CCTV cameras. It's a warehouse store for the restaurant trade, offering every imaginable appliance and vessel. Shelf after shelf is piled high with pans, skillets, steamers, hotpots, baking dishes and gleaming tinware. There are elaborate cake stands, fantastical jelly-moulds, and an entire aisle of woks. Tiny woks for flash-frying individual prawns, jacuzzi-sized woks capacious enough for a whole ox.

The place has only a handful of customers. There's a young couple quietly arguing about kebab-skewers, a harassed-looking man loading a trolley with bamboo dim-sum steamers, and an elderly woman muttering to herself as she picks through the melon-ballers.

In the last aisle, Villanelle finds what she's looking for. Cleavers. Fine-bladed cleavers for slicing and dicing, heavy bone-choppers for hacking and dismembering. Her eye alights on a *chukabocho*, a locally made cleaver with a 25oz carbon-steel blade and a tiger-maple handle. It feels good in her hand. Two minutes later she checks out, paying for a dozen cocktail glasses and several sets of paper umbrellas.

Somehow, unseen by the CCTV cameras, the *chukabocho* has made its way to the bottom of her shoulder bag.

'OK, I admit it,' says Eve. 'I'm nervous.'

'You've been on dates before, haven't you?'

'This is not a date. This is an appointment with the head of the Chinese Secret Service.'

'If you say so. I think he fancies you.'

'Simon, please. You're not helping. I feel very uncomfortable in this dress. And these shoes. I can hardly walk.'

'You look adorable. When are you meeting him?'

'He's picking me up downstairs in ten minutes. What are your plans?'

'I thought I might take a stroll down the Bund.' He shrugs. 'Perhaps look in somewhere for a cocktail.'

'Well, be good. I'm going to wait downstairs.'

'Have fun.'

She throws him a sardonic glance, and teetering a little in her new Lilian Zhang cocktail dress and Mary Ching stilettos – the prospect of submitting the expenses claim makes her blood run cold – runs a last check in the mirror. She looks, she's forced to admit, pretty good. The hotel hairdresser's even magicked her unruly hair into something resembling a French roll.

'You don't think the make-up's too much?'

'No! Now *go*.'

The invitation came as a surprise, to say the least. The meeting in the Peninsula suite had more or less stalled after Eve's questioning of Jin Qiang. Spies, even among themselves, are highly disinclined to admit that they actively engage in spying. Following a further hour of discussion of the murder of Zhang Lei, in the course of which Eve handed over a prepared dossier about the investigation of the Kedrin murder, Jin brought the meeting to a halt and ushered her and Simon down to the lobby.

There, amid the art deco grandeur, the same cast of business types appeared to be engaged in the same muted conversations. As they shook hands beneath the pillared portico, Jin hesitated. 'Mrs Polastri, I'd very much like to show you something of Shanghai. Are you by any chance free this evening?'

'I am,' she said, surprised.

'Excellent. I'll call for you at your hotel at eight o'clock.'

She opened her mouth to thank him, but he was already gliding soundlessly away.

He arrives at 8 p.m. precisely. He's on a scooter, wearing a sharp black suit and open-necked white shirt, and looks a very different man from the cautious intelligence officer Eve met just hours earlier.

'Mrs Polastri, you look . . . spectacular.' With a courtly smile he hands her a tiny bouquet of fresh violets, tied with a silk ribbon.

Eve is enchanted, and thinking of Niko teaching GCSE maths to a class of bored teenagers half a world away, she feels a stab of guilt. Thanking Jin, she wraps the dewy violets in a tissue and places them in her bag.

'Ready?' he asks, passing her a helmet.

'Ready.' She arranges herself side-saddle, as she's seen Shanghainese women do.

They swing out into the traffic, and onto East Nanjing Road. The thoroughfare, one of Shanghai's busiest, is gridlocked and exhaust-choked. Jin weaves the scooter deftly between the crawling vehicles and comes to a halt at a red light.

As Eve sits there, the scooter burbling beneath her, she catches sight of a striking figure walking up the pavement towards her. A young woman, poised and slender, in jeans and a black, pearl-buttoned cardigan. Dark blonde hair slicked back from fine, sharp-cut features. A subtle, sensual twist to the mouth.

Eve watches her for a moment. Has she seen that face before, or is it just déjà vu? As if sensing her stare, the woman glances back. She's beautiful, in the way that a bird of prey is beautiful, but never has Eve encountered a gaze of such inhuman blankness. When the lights change, and the scooter lurches forward, the temperature seems to have dropped a degree or two.

Five minutes later they draw up at an intersection, outside a grand art deco building topped by a cascading neon spire. Coloured lights course up and down its antique facade. Above the portico, the word *Paramount* blazes into the twilight.

'You like dancing?'

'I . . . yes,' Eve replies. 'I do, actually.'

'The Paramount is a famous landmark from the nineteen-thirties. This is where everyone came to dance. Gangsters, high society, beautiful women . . .'

She smiles. 'You sound as if you'd like those days to return.'

He locks the scooter. 'They were interesting times. But then so are these. Come.'

She accompanies him into a foyer hung with sepia photographs, and from there into a small lift that conveys them unhurriedly to the fourth floor. The dance hall is like a music box in gilt and red plush. On the stage, a middle-aged singer in a floor-length evening dress is delivering a smoky-voiced version of 'Bye Bye Blackbird', as a dozen or so couples gravely quickstep around the cantilevered dance floor.

Jin leads Eve to a side table in a booth, and orders Coca-Cola for both of them.

'Business first?' he asks.

'Business first,' she agrees, sipping the sugary drink. A couple glides wordlessly past them.

'What I tell you, you never repeat, OK?'

She shakes her head. 'This conversation never took place. We talked about dancing. About nightlife in Old Shanghai.'

He moves closer to her on the banquette, and inclines his head towards hers. 'Our late friend, as you know, was killed in an establishment in the Old City. He was a surgery fetishist. A masochist. We knew about this. He visited the place every six weeks or so, and paid a professional sex worker to simulate . . . various medical procedures. He was discreet about these visits; his colleagues knew nothing about them.'

'But not discreet enough to escape your department's notice, evidently.'

'Evidently.'

Eve notes that Jin is, in effect, admitting that Zhang Lei was working for the state.

'So we are either looking at an organisation able to mount an extensive and long-term surveillance operation . . .' She hesitates. 'Or one with access to information acquired by your department.'

146

Jin frowns. 'Certainly the former. Just conceivably the latter.'

Eve nods slowly. 'Either way, a sophisticated organisation with a long reach.'

'Yes. And I don't believe it was the British, or the Americans. The economic consequences of discovery would be . . .'

'Catastrophic?' Eve suggests.

'Yes. That's right.'

'So do you have any other ideas for who might be responsible?'

'Right now, not really, although one can never discount a Russian connection, especially if, as you suggest, the same organisation is responsible for the death of Viktor Kedrin. So we're trying very hard to find out more about the woman they sent. We know that she entered by the back stairway, overpowered the sex worker who calls herself Nurse Wu, who remembers nothing beyond the fact that her attacker was a woman, and then eliminated our friend by means of carbon monoxide poisoning.'

'You're sure that was the cause of death? It couldn't have been an accident on the part of this nurse person. After all, she wasn't qualified to administer surgical gas or anything of the sort, surely.'

'The only gas she ever gave her "patients" was pure oxygen. We tested all the tanks there. And as it happens, as well as being a part-time sex-worker she was also a trained nurse, who worked in a private medical facility in Pudong. So she knew what she was doing. And the symptoms of carbon monoxide poisoning are unmistakable.'

'Cherry-red lips and skin?'

'Exactly. The pathologist was in no doubt.'

'But no sign of a CO tank, or canister?'

'No, the killer took it away with her.'

'And what makes this Wu person so sure that her attacker was a woman?'

'She remembers the feel of a woman's breasts against her back when she was grabbed. And the hand that went over her mouth was strong, she said, but not a man's hand.'

'She's sure about this?'

'Very sure. And there's a man who has a food stall on Dangfeng Road opposite the backstairs exit. He knows what the building is, and that only men come out of that door. So when he saw a woman, he remembered her.'

'Does he remember what she looked like?'

'No, he said all Westerners look the same to him. Baseball cap is all he remembers. New York Yankees.'

'Our killer's very good at being invisible. Has the material on the Kedrin murder been any use?'

'Very much so. My service is very grateful, Mrs Polastri. We showed the images of the woman in the hotel to people who work on Dangfeng Road, and several said they might have seen her that day.'

'But no one was sure?'

'No. Unfortunately.'

'They're very poor quality images. And you can't see her face. So I'm not surprised.'

'We are grateful, nevertheless. And of course we're checking against visas, and watching all border points. We're talking to people in all the hotels, clubs, and restaurants that a foreigner might visit.'

'I'm sure you're doing everything that could be done.'

'We are.' Jin smiles. 'And now, would you like to dance?'

Dragon-fruit Martini in hand, Simon makes his way towards one of the Star Bar's few unoccupied seats, which appears to be upholstered in zebra-skin. 'Boss Ass Bitch' by Nicki Minaj is pumping from concealed speakers, and the place is filling fast. Simon is wearing Diesel jeans and a cotton jacket, and the Lonely Planet guide from which he chose the bar ('a watering-hole popular with the cashed-up expat crowd') is weighing down his right-hand pocket.

He would never admit it to Eve, and obviously she's his head of section and it's Jin Qiang's turf, but he's not exactly happy that she's swanned off without him for a night on the town with Jin. It's not as if she's not going to tell him everything that's discussed when she gets back, but it would have been nice if she'd, at the very least, *suggested* that he come along. He's very fond of Eve in an exasperated, semi-protective sort of way (her fashion sense, oh my *God*) and he certainly isn't one of those sad haters who can't deal with a female boss, but she can be pretty insensitive at times, despite her undoubtedly high-wattage intellect.

Lowering himself into the zebra-skin chair with an insouciance he doesn't feel, Simon takes a deep hit of his drink. The Star Bar's decor is preposterous, even for Shanghai. The emerald-green stingray-skin walls are hung with sub-pornographic paintings, the fireplace is black marble, a vast Fortuny-style chandelier glows overhead. The overall effect is absurd, alluring, vaguely satanic.

The Martini is volcanically strong, caressing Simon's taste buds with sugary top notes before drenching his

149

cerebellum in iced Berry Bros. No 3 gin. Half-closing his eyes, he feels himself wreathed in flavour. Juniper, a hint of grapefruit, and that sexy, suggestive dragon-fruit sweetness. *Fuck me*, he murmurs, his brain clouding with pleasure. *That hits the spot*. Around him drift expensively dressed revellers. Friends, office colleagues, lovers ... Why is it always, *always* like this? Everyone else at ease, having the time of their overpaid lives, while he's on the outside, face pressed to the glass, invisible.

'All alone?'

At first Simon takes no notice, not believing that the question has been addressed to him. Then the slight, dark-haired figure at his side swims into focus. He takes in the mischievous upturned eyes, the dimpled grin, the sharp little teeth.

'I suppose I am, yes.'

'You new here then. I think I remember if I see you before.'

'My name's Simon. I got in a couple of days ago.' He gazes at her, marvelling at the soft swell of her breasts in the lilac crop-top, the trim little stomach, the skinny jeans and pretty, strappy shoes. She is, without question, the most beautiful creature he's ever seen.

'Hi,' she says. 'I'm Janie.'

Jin Qiang is a superb dancer. To the swooping, shivering strains of 'Moon River', he waltzes Eve expertly round the floor, one hand lightly holding hers, the other against the bare flesh of her back, guiding her. Despite their price, she's glad she bought the cocktail dress and the shoes.

'So would you like to have lived in the 1930s?' she asks him.

'It was a time of great inequality. Great hardship for many.'

'I know. But also elegance . . . glamour.'

'Are you familiar with Chinese cinema, Mrs Polastri?'

'No, I'm afraid not.'

'There's a film I love, made here in Shanghai in the 1930s, called *The Goddess*. A silent film. Very sad. Very beautiful and tragic actress Ruan Lingyu. She shows great emotion in her face, and in her movements.'

'She sounds wonderful.'

'She killed herself, aged twenty-four. She was unhappy in love.'

'Oh my goodness, that is tragic.'

'Indeed. Today, I don't think many people in Shanghai would kill themselves for love. Too busy making money.'

'You sound like a romantic, Mr Jin?'

'There are a few of us left. But we operate in secret.'

'Like spies?' Eve suggests.

They both smile, and 'Moon River' comes to a close. Ice-blue neon flickers round the stage, and the singer segues into 'The Girl from Ipanema'.

'The foxtrot,' says Jin. 'My favourite.'

'I'm sorry you're stuck with me. With my two left feet.'

'You have two left feet? Really?'

'It's an expression. It means I'm a bit clumsy.'

'That is something I would never say about you, Mrs Polastri.'

Half an hour later they're on the scooter again, careering through streets vivid with neon. Eve is enjoying herself. Jin is a man of many interests. Hunan food, early Chinese cinema, and post-punk music among them. His favourite band, he tells her, is Gang of Four. 'With that name, how could I resist them?' At the same time Eve recognises that for all the wry surface charm, there is a steeliness to Jin Qiang. In a tight corner, this man would make the hard choice, take the pragmatic decision.

They come to a halt outside an unprepossessing-looking establishment on a side street. As Jin opens the door, oily steam gusts into their faces. The place is crammed, and noise levels are deafening. Everyone seems to be shouting, and there's a continuous clattering of pans and woks from the kitchen. Standing in the doorway, Eve is pushed roughly out of the way by a departing customer. Taking her arm, Jin steers her towards the small counter. A tiny, ancient woman in a greasy apron appears and directs them to a plastic-topped table. Narrowing her eyes at Eve, she screeches at Jin in Mandarin.

'She says I'm a very naughty boy,' he tells Eve. 'She thinks I've picked you up.'

She laughs. 'You're going to have to help me with the menu.'

He inspects the streamers pinned to the walls. 'How about bullfrog in rice wine?'

In the end they settle for spicy skewered shrimps and cumin-crusted ribs washed down with cold beer. It's delicious, among the best food Eve has ever tasted. 'Thank you,' she says, when she can eat no more. 'That was fantastic.'

'Not bad,' he agrees. 'And private.'

She knows what he means. Given the noise levels, audio surveillance would be impossible here.

'I have something for you,' he says, and below the level of the table, places a sealed envelope on her lap.

She doesn't move or speak.

'I'm trusting you with my career, Mrs Polastri. If you are right, and we face a common enemy – this organisation you speak of – we should work together. But I doubt Beijing would see it that way, so . . .'

'I understand,' says Eve quietly. 'And thank you. We will not let you down.'

Simon knows, straight away. Janie's hands, perhaps. Something in the set of her cheekbones and her mouth. But it doesn't matter. He's lost.

She tells him she works for a child-minding agency. That she lives in a one-bedroom flat in Jingan, near the Art Theatre. As they talk she gazes at him. No one's ever looked at him like this. The soft, unblinking stare. The long brown eyes fixed patiently on his.

There was a girl at university, an Eng Lit student who played in a ukelele band. She and Simon slept together intermittently, but he was never quite sure what she expected from him, and eventually the relationship faded into a friendship with which they were both more comfortable. He wondered, vaguely, if he was gay, and in the spirit of experiment, allowed himself to be seduced by his male tutor, a mediaevalist with a penchant for Gregorian plainchant and spanking. That didn't really work out either, and Simon decided to let the whole sex thing slide, and to concentrate on his studies. He left with a first-class degree and an unfocused sense of longing. For what or for whom, he didn't know. For almost a year he lived at home, celibate and unemployed. Then one day, almost as a joke, a friend emailed him a link to MI5's recruitment page. From day one, the secret world felt like home.

He's told Janie that he's 'here on business', and this seems to satisfy her. She asks him about his likes and dislikes. About movies he's seen, about pop videos, boy-bands, celebrities, shopping and fashion. In anyone else this bubblegum worldview would be exasperating. In Janie, it's enchanting.

Two dragon-fruit Martinis later (Sprite for her, touchingly), they're dancing. The playlist is commercial pop, and Janie sings along to every track. Simon's not much of a dancer, but the floor's too crowded to do more than shuffle and nod. The tempo slows, and he places his hands on her hips, feeling their gentle sway, inhaling the scent of the jasmine blooms pinned to her upswept hair. Intoxicated, he draws her towards him, and she lays her head on his shoulder. Through his jacket, which he dares not remove for fear that it will be stolen, he feels the unyielding pressure of her breasts. His heart pounding, he touches his lips to the soft tendrils of hair at her temple. He doesn't think she'll sense this but she does, and her face tilts up to his, her lips parted.

Kissing her, feeling the sugary flicker of her tongue, he feels a lightness of being so intense he wonders if he's going to pass out. She moves her mouth across his cheek, nips his earlobe with her little cat's teeth. 'You know I wasn't always a girl,' she whispers.

He knows. He can feel the evidence swelling against his thigh.

'It's fine, Janie,' he says. 'Really, it's fine.'

154

Back at the Sea Bird Hotel, Eve knocks on Simon's door, but he's still out. And having a good time, she hopes. He's a good friend and colleague, but he definitely needs to loosen up.

In her room, she takes out the envelope that Jin has given her. Inside is a single A4 page, which appears to be a print-out of a transfer of funds between two international banks. The banks and account-holders are identified only by number codes. The sum in question is a little over £17 million.

Eve stares at the paper for a moment, trying to divine its importance, before replacing it in its envelope and locking it in her briefcase. Jin, she knows, is returning to Beijing tomorrow. The investigation into Zhang Lei's murder will continue, but there is no more that she can contribute. It's time for her and Simon to fly back to London, report to Richard Edwards, and investigate the lead that Jin has given her at such personal risk. She also needs, urgently, to make things right with Niko. It will be good to be home again, but part of her will miss Shanghai and its luxurious strangeness, its myriad scents and colours. And part of her, she's forced to admit, will miss Jin Qiang.

In bed, she reviews the evening moment by moment, and in particular the dancing. The open window admits a faint breeze, and with it the corrupt tang of Suzhou Creek. It takes her some time to fall asleep.

Drifting between wakefulness and dream, Simon knows a peace that he's never thought possible. Beside him, Janie turns, and raises her arms sleepily above her head. 'Promise you like me?' she murmurs. 'Not just using for sex? Wham-bam, then bye-bye Janie?'

'Like you?' he wants to tell her. '*I love you*. You're everything I've ever wanted. I'd give up my work, my country, everything I know and believe in, to share my life with you.' But he says nothing, and instead plants slow kisses on the pale curve of her left breast. She watches him for a moment, and then, eyelids fluttering, she plucks at her nipples and they begin again.

Some time later Simon wakes, and through half-closed eyes sees her tiptoeing round the room, slim-hipped and naked, long hair swinging round her shoulders. When she first brought him here, he was touched by the modesty of the place. The cheap chest of drawers and dressing table, the Barbie-pink curtains and bedspread, the Hello Kitty poster on the wall. Now she touches his clothes, running her fingers over the jacket he's slung over the single chair. A slim hand disappears, and an instant later reappears holding his phone. She looks at it admiringly for a couple of seconds, and replaces it. The action touches Simon, who guesses that such an article is way beyond her budget.

Then, with great speed, she dresses herself, pulling on white knickers, jeans and a T-shirt, and pushing her feet into a pair of trainers. As she tip-toes towards Simon, he pretends to be asleep. She leans over him for a moment, so close that he can hear her breath, and then backs soundlessly away. Opening his eyes, he sees her dip her hand back into his jacket, take the phone, and hurry from the room.

Simon lies there for a moment, too shocked to move. Then he leaps from the bed, and lifts the rattan blind. He catches a fleeting glimpse of Janie beneath a street light, moving fast, and then she's gone.

He pulls his clothes on, sick with dread, and races down the narrow staircase to the street. It's rained while they've been in bed, and the air is charged with the smell of the wet streets. Simon is soon breathless and footsore, his shirt clammy with sweat.

But there she is ahead, and he drives himself after her. What the fuck? *What the actual fuck?* Has he just fallen hook, line and sinker for the oldest scam in the book? If Eve and Richard Edwards discover any of this, *any* of it, he's finished. Forget the sheer, gobsmacking unprofessionalism, the humiliation would be off the scale. Honey-trapped by a nightclub tranny. A chick with a dick. What a 24-carat twat he's going to look.

There's just one chance. If he can get to her, and somehow get his phone back . . . Perhaps, just perhaps, Janie's exactly what she says she is. Perhaps she simply couldn't resist the chance to make a few bucks by stealing a high-tech foreign phone. Please, he prays, as he dodges and weaves through the crowds, dragging the muggy night air into his lungs, *please* let that be the case. Let it be something forgivable. Let me get back with Janie. Because he knows that as long as he lives, he will never experience anything like the dreamy bliss of their intertwined limbs.

The streets are narrowing now, and the crowds thinning. Instead of street lights, there are loops of low-wattage bulbs strung between half-completed dwellings. Incurious faces look up from beneath sagging awnings and watch him as he passes. There are still a few food stalls operating, a few woks sizzling over charcoal fires, and Simon slows to avoid a rickety table supporting a plastic bowl of writhing, living creatures.

Janie's still about forty yards ahead – Christ, she can move – and now they're in some kind of new-build estate. Rendered-brick housing blocks intersected by a grid of unlit lanes. The area's almost deserted, and if she turns now, she'll see him.

Shrinking into the shadows Simon checks his watch. It's almost 2 a.m. The temptation to call out to Janie is agonising, overwhelming. But he has to know the truth.

At the entrance to one of the buildings she presses a buzzer. After perhaps half a minute, a figure steps into the dim pool of light, and Simon knows immediately that the scenario is infinitely worse than any he's imagined. The man's not Chinese. He looks Russian or Eastern European, and he's got hardcore intelligence operative written all over him. Even at a distance, he radiates a pitiless authority. I'm fucked, Simon tells himself, as Janie hands the man the MI6-issue phone. I'm totally and utterly fucked.

Too wretched to be afraid, he forces himself to note every detail of the man's appearance. There's a brief conversation, and then he and Janie vanish into the building together. After a minute, Simon warily approaches the entrance, looking for a name or a number. There doesn't appear to be either, but he's confident he will be able to find the place again.

Briefly, he considers simply telling Eve that he has lost his phone, that it's been stolen, and not saying anything about Janie. But he knows that it's not in him to lie. He'll tell her everything and offer his resignation, effective immediately. Perhaps she'll accept it and send him back to London for what will undoubtedly be a highly unpleasant debriefing by Richard Edwards. Perhaps – and his heart leaps sadly at the prospect – they'll decide to keep him in play. Feed him back to Janie to find out who's running her.

He's fifty metres from the building when he hears his name called.

He stops, sure that he's mistaken. But there it is again, low and clear on the warm, damp air. Is it Janie? How could it be? As far as she's concerned, he's asleep in her flat.

'Simon, over here.'

The voice is coming from the unlit lane on his left. Heart pounding, he takes half-a-dozen tentative steps, senses movement in the darkness, catches an incongruous hint of French perfume on the night air.

'Who's there?' he asks, his voice unsteady.

He has a momentary impression of a figure exploding from the shadows, of the whirling arc of the *chukabocho*, and then the carbon steel blade chops through his throat with such force that his head is almost severed.

Rising on her toes like a matador, eyes demonic, Villanelle sidesteps the black swathe of blood thrown from the falling body. Simon's limbs shudder, a bubbling sound issues from his neck, and as he dies Villanelle feels a rush of feeling so intense, so icily numbing, it almost brings her to her knees. She crouches there for a moment, waves of sensation coursing through her. Then, wrenching the *chukabocho* free of the corpse and dropping it into a plastic shopping bag, followed by her bloodied surgical gloves, she walks swiftly away.

Ten minutes later she spots a battered Kymco scooter parked at the foot of an apartment block. Disabling the ignition lock and kick-starting the engine, she heads north-wards, keeping to the narrower roads, until she reaches

Nan Suzhou Lu, where she drops the plastic bag into the dark swirl of the creek. It's a beautiful night – the sky purple, the city dim gold – and Villanelle feels vibrantly, thrillingly alive. Killing the English spy has restored something in her. The Zhang Lei action had its professional satisfactions, but the moment itself lacked impact. Taking out Simon Mortimer was a return to first principles. A violent, artistic kill. The *chukabocho*, weighed in the hand, was not so very different from the Spetsnaz machete her father taught her to use when she was a teenager. Unwieldy to begin with, but a lethal thing when correctly deployed.

The beauty of it is, she had no choice. Konstantin had ordered Janie to make sure that she was never followed to a rendezvous, and to drug the Englishman if necessary. But the little hooker fucked up, and once Simon Mortimer saw Konstantin, he couldn't be allowed to live. That's the way she's going to argue it, anyway. The killing will almost certainly be blamed on the Triads, whose traditional murder weapon is the cleaver. Polastri will get the message loud and clear, but as far as everyone else is concerned – the press, the police – Simon Mortimer's just going to be a tourist who found himself in the wrong place, at the wrong time.

Villanelle is about to head southwards towards the French Concession when a thought occurs to her. Within minutes, the scooter is puttering to a halt at the foot of a building adjacent to the Sea Bird Hotel. The hotel is unlit except for a small blue neon sign over the entrance. Villanelle knows which room is Eve's; Konstantin's surveillance people have watched her come and go since the night she and Simon arrived.

Silently, Villanelle climbs up the side of the hotel, the antique pipework and ironwork balconies offering easy hand- and footholds even in the near-darkness, and slips feet-first through the open, third-floor window.

For almost two minutes she crouches there, unmoving. Then she steps soundlessly towards the bed.

Eve's clothes have been hung over a chair, and Villanelle gently runs the back of her hand over the black silk cocktail dress before lifting it to her face. It smells, very faintly, of scent, perspiration and traffic-fumes.

Eve's lying with her mouth slightly open and one arm flung across the pillow. She's wearing a flesh-coloured camisole, and without make-up looks unexpectedly vulnerable. Kneeling beside her, Villanelle listens to the whisper of her breath, and inhales her warm smell. Noting the faint tremor of Eve's mouth, she touches her tongue to her own upper lip which has begun, very faintly, to throb.

'My enemy,' she murmurs in Russian, touching Eve's hair. '*Moy vrag.*'

Almost as an afterthought, she searches the room. There's a combination-locked briefcase chained to the bed she decides to leave alone. But on the bedside table, there's a pretty, gilt-clasped eternity bracelet, and this Villanelle takes.

'Thank you,' she whispers, and with a last look at Eve slips silently out of the window. As she goes she hears the distant siren of an ambulance and the whooping of police cars. But Eve, for now, does not stir.

It's five weeks later, and at midday the grey sky over the Dever Research Station promises rain. Set in sixty acres outside the village of Bullington in Hampshire, the former

Logistics Corps barracks appears from the outside to comprise little more than a cluster of dilapidated red-brick blocks and prefabricated huts. Chain-link fencing topped with razor wire and signs prohibiting photography lend the place a grimly uninviting aspect.

Despite its neglected air Dever is an active station, classified as a top-secret government asset. Among other functions, it acts as a base for E Squadron, a Special Forces unit whose role is to conduct deniable operations in support of the Secret Intelligence Service.

Identifying himself at the gatehouse, Richard Edwards parks his thirty-year-old S-class Mercedes on an area of cracked tarmac. With the exception of a couple of security personnel who are making an unhurried circuit of the perimeter, the place appears deserted. Making his way past the main administration block, Richard enters a low, windowless building. Descending to the underground firing range, he finds Eve field-stripping a Glock 19 pistol under the watchful eye of Calum Dennis, the station armourer.

'So how are we doing?' he enquires, when the slide, spring, barrel, frame and magazine have been neatly lined up on the gun-mat.

'Getting there,' says Calum.

Eve stares fixedly down the range. 'Can I try that last drill again?'

'Sure,' says Calum, handing Richard a pair of ear-defenders.

'Ready when you are,' says Eve, putting on her own ear-defenders.

Calum types a series of instructions into a laptop, and as he hits Enter, the range is plunged into darkness. Fifteen seconds pass, during which the only sound is the sigh of the ventilators and a metallic clicking as Eve assembles the Glock. Then a target, a human torso, is briefly illuminated at the far end of the range and she snaps off two shots, the muzzle flash bright in the darkness. Four more static targets appear, and Eve fires paired shots at each. The final target moves from side to side, and she discharges the last five rounds in her magazine in fast succession.

'Well . . .' Calum says and smiles faintly, lowering a pair of binoculars. 'His afternoon's fucked.'

Outside, an hour later, Eve's walking Richard back to his car. Rain's falling in a thin mist, shining her hair.

'You don't have to do any of this,' he tells her. 'By rights, I should take you off this investigation. Sort you out with an official position in the Service.'

'It's too late, Richard. That woman killed Simon, and I want her for it.'

'You don't know that. The police report said it was almost certainly a Triad hit, and we know that Janie Chou person he hooked up with had links to organised crime.'

'Richard, please, don't treat me like an idiot, the Triads don't chop up tourists. That bitch killed Simon just as surely as she killed Kedrin and the others. I saw his body, she almost beheaded him.'

He unlocks the Mercedes. Stands there for a moment, head bowed. 'Promise me one thing, Eve. That if you find her, you won't go anywhere near her. And I mean anywhere.'

She looks away, expressionless.

'That weapon you insist on carrying. Don't go thinking that a couple of decent groupings on the range gives you any kind of licence to take chances. It doesn't.'

163

'Richard, the reason that I've spent the last ten days here at Dever is that she knows who I am. Killing Simon was a message, addressed to me. She was saying: I can take you, and the people you care about, *any fucking time I want . . .*' Eve pats the Glock, now holstered at her side. 'I've seen what she can do, and I need to be ready, it's that simple.'

He shakes his head. 'I should never have got you involved. It was a grave mistake.'

'Well, I am involved. And the only way that this thing is ever going to end is if we find her and kill her. So please let me get on with that.'

As she walks back towards the range, Richard watches her go. Then he climbs into the Mercedes, switches on the ignition and the windscreen wipers, and begins the drive back to London.

4

Villanelle wakes in a warm tangle of limbs. On the far side of the bed Anne-Laure is lying face down, her hair a honey-coloured swirl, one suntanned arm trailing across Kim's chest. Where Anne-Laure is all dreamy curves, Kim displays a lynx-like elegance, even in sleep. His features are lean and refined, reflecting his Franco-Vietnamese ancestry, and his limbs are the colour of ivory, their musculature precisely defined in the morning light.

Detaching herself, Villanelle walks to the bathroom, and takes a shower. Still naked, she pads to the tiny galley kitchen, fills the Bialetti coffee maker with Hédiard's 'Sur la Côte d'Azur' blend, and switches on the ceramic hob. At the end of the kitchen a sliding glass door leads to a small terrace, and Villanelle steps outside for a moment. It's September, and Paris is radiant with the dying summer. The horizon is a pale haze, pigeons are cooing on a neighbouring rooftop, and the faint murmur of traffic rises from the rue de Vaugirard, six storeys below.

Anne-Laure inherited the single-bedroom apartment five months ago, and tells her husband, Gilles, a senior functionary at the Treasury, that she goes there 'to write' and 'to think'. If Gilles thinks this out of character, and suspects that the place is put to more active use, he doesn't say so, because he himself has recently taken a mistress. His secretary, to be precise, a plain and unstylish woman with whom he cannot be seen socially, but who, unlike Anne-Laure, never questions or criticises him.

Villanelle stands there, gazing out over the city, until she hears the rasp of the percolating coffee. In the bedroom, Anne-Laure is stirring, her fingers sleepily re-acquainting themselves with the hard contours of Kim's body. He is twenty-three, and a dancer at the Paris Opera Ballet. Anne-Laure and Villanelle met him twelve hours earlier at a drinks party given by a fashion designer. It took them just three minutes to persuade him to leave with them.

Anne-Laure is astride Kim now, her hands braced against his muscular thighs, her eyes half-closed. Setting the coffee tray down on a bedside table, Villanelle clears the chaise longue of discarded clothes and arranges herself, cat-like, on the soft brocade. She likes watching her friend having sex, but this morning there's an artificial quality to Anne-Laure's gasping and sighing and hair-tossing. It's a performance, and from his blank expression and the dutiful bucking of his hips, Villanelle can tell that Kim isn't buying it.

Catching his eye, Villanelle hitches her knees up, spreads her thighs, and begins, very slowly and deliberately, to finger herself. Anne-Laure is oblivious to this performance, but Kim stares intently between her legs. Villanelle returns his gaze, notes his anguished look as he tries to hold himself back, and watches as he shudders to a climax. Seconds later, with a plaintive cry, Anne-Laure subsides on top of him.

On the chaise longue Villanelle stretches and licks her finger. Sex, for her, offers only fleeting physical satisfaction.

What she finds much more exciting is to look into another person's eyes and to know, like a cobra swaying in front of its hypnotised prey, that she is in absolute control. But that game gets boring, too. People capitulate so easily.

'Coffee, anyone?' she enquires.

Half an hour later Kim has left for ballet class at the Opera and Villanelle and Anne-Laure are sitting outside on the terrace. Anne-Laure's wearing a silk kimono, while Villanelle's in cigarette jeans and a Miu Miu sweater, her hair twisted into a scrappy chignon. Both are barefoot.

'So, does Gilles still fuck you?' Villanelle asks.

'From time to time,' says Anne-Laure. She takes a cigarette from the packet beside her and flicks her gold Dunhill lighter. 'He probably thinks that if he stops altogether I'll suspect something.'

They fall silent. Before them is the roofscape of the Sixième Arrondissement, tranquil in the morning light. It's a luxury to be able to sit like this, chasing the morning away with inconsequential chatter, and both women know it. Six storeys below, people are racing to work, fighting for taxis, and jamming themselves into buses and Metro carriages. Anne-Laure and Villanelle's financial needs are well taken care of, so they're free to abstain from this daily grind. Free to pick through vintage clothes stores in the Marais, lunch at yam'Tcha or Le Cristal, and have their hair done by Tom at Carita.

Over London, a leaden sky promises rain. In her office above Goodge Street Underground station, Eve Polastri wrenches a wad of printing paper from the photocopier and repositions it, but the paper-jam light continues to blink.

'And sod you, too,' she mutters, punching the off button.

Eve's using the fifteen-year-old copier because the scanner's given up the ghost and is now lying unplugged on the floor, where sooner or later she's going to trip over it. She's put in a request for new office equipment, or at least a budget for repairs, and there have been vague promises from Vauxhall Cross, but given the byzantine arrangement by which the operation is funded, she's not hopeful.

Today, Eve is to be joined by two new colleagues, both male. Richard Edwards has described them as 'an enterprising couple of blokes', which could mean anything. At a guess, a pair of low-flyers with discipline issues who have failed to adjust to the ordered, hierarchical world of the Secret Intelligence Service. Whatever their history, they're unlikely to regard Goodge Street as a promotion.

Eve glances at the battered metal desk formerly occupied by her deputy. A scattering of effects – a Thermos flask, a Kylie Minogue mug filled with pens, a Disney 'Frozen' snow-globe – stands as he left them, untouched. Seeing this dusty array, Eve feels a vast weariness. There was a time when her mission was straightforward, and its purposes clearly defined. Now, three months after Simon's murder, a paralysing uncertainty bears down on her. The outlines of her task, once so hard-edged, have dissolved into a blur, as indistinct as the view through the grime-streaked office window.

She wonders, vaguely, if she should have taken more care with her appearance. She's wearing a zip-up tracksuit top, a pair of baggy-arsed supermarket jeans, and trainers. Simon was always on at her to make a bit more of herself, but all that vanity stuff – shopping, make-up, hairdressing

– doesn't come naturally to her. When she was working with the Joint Services Analysis Group at Thames House, a well-meaning colleague took her for an afternoon at an expensive spa. Eve tried to enjoy herself, but she was bored witless. It all seemed so unimportant.

One of the things she's always loved about Niko is that none of these things matter to him, either. Yet he makes her feel beautiful, and sometimes, at the most ordinary of moments – when she's getting dressed, perhaps, or climbing out of the bath – she catches him gazing at her with a tenderness that pierces her to the heart.

For how much longer, she wonders, will he look at her like that. How unreasonably will she have to behave for him to wake up one morning and decide that he just can't continue? They must be almost at that point already. She's taken to pacing mutely around the flat in the evenings, vodka-tonic in hand, like an alcoholic ghost. Later, as often as not, she passes out in front of her laptop. Murdered men stalk her dreams, and she wakes at random hours of the night, her heart pounding with dread.

Lance Pope and Billy Primrose arrive at 10 a.m., and exchange unreadable glances as Eve introduces herself. Lance is fortyish, with the lean, suspicious features of a stoat. Billy, audibly wheezing after the climb up the stairs, looks barely out of his teens, with black-dyed hair, skin like suet, and a deathly back-bedroom pallor.

'So this is it,' Lance murmurs.

Eve nods. 'A long way from the comforts of Vauxhall Cross, I'm afraid.'

'I've spent most of my career in the field. I'm not choosy about furniture.'

'Just as well.'

'I've ordered some hardware,' says Billy, still wheezing faintly. 'External processors, logic and protocol analysers. Basic stuff.'

'Good luck with that. I filed a requisition order six weeks ago.'

'It'll be here this afternoon. I'll need a bit of space.'

'Well, help yourself.' She takes off her glasses and rubs her eyes. 'How much do you both know about why you're here?'

'Bugger all,' says Lance. 'We were told you'd brief us.'

She replaces her glasses, and the two men swim back into focus. Billy in gothic black, Lance in a seedy version of sports casual. She finds them both deeply unprepossessing, confirming the impression she gained from their files.

At seventeen, using the online handle '$qeeky', a reference to the asthma from which he'd suffered since childhood, Billy was a member of a hacker collective responsible for a series of well-publicised attacks on corporate and government websites. The FBI and Interpol eventually took the group down, and its leaders received prison sentences, but the underage Billy was released on bail on the condition that he live at home, under curfew, with no access to the Internet. Within weeks he had been recruited by MI6's Security Exploitation team.

Lance is a career MI6 officer, and a veteran of numerous overseas postings. Although an experienced agent runner, commended by the heads of station he has served under, he has not been promoted in several years. The problem is his chronic insolvency, caused by a predilection for online gambling. He's divorced, and lives alone in a one-room rented flat in Croydon.

'We're here to hunt down a professional assassin,' Eve tells them. 'We have no name, no country of origin, no information concerning political affiliation. We know that she is a woman, probably in her mid- to late-twenties, and that she acts on behalf of an extremely well-resourced organisation with a global reach. We know that she's got at least six high-profile kills to her name.'

Rain begins to beat at the office window, and she zips her tracksuit top up to her chin. 'There are two main reasons we need to catch this woman, apart from the fact that she's a serial murderer who needs to be stopped.'

'Which isn't the concern of the Service,' says Lance, almost to himself.

'Which wouldn't normally be our concern, but in this case, very much is. I'm assuming you both know who I mean by Viktor Kedrin?'

Billy nods. 'Fascist nut-job, Russian, taken out in London last year.' He scratches his groin absent-mindedly. 'Weren't Moscow behind that?'

'The SVR? No, that's what everyone assumed. In fact Kedrin and his bodyguards were shot dead by our target. It was a brutally efficient job, and she carried it out alone.'

'You're sure about that?' asks Lance.

'Absolutely. And for what it's worth, we have a CCTV image of her.' Eve hands each man a printout of a blurry figure in a parka, with the hood up. The image has been captured from behind. She could be anyone.

'Best we've got?' asks Lance.

Eve nods, and hands them each another printout. 'But she may resemble this woman. Lucy Drake.'

Billy gives a low whistle. 'Pretty fit, then.'

'Lucy Drake's a model. Our killer used her as a double, to check into Kedrin's hotel and to approach him in a lecture hall. But the likeness may only be superficial.'

'So could she have been freelancing for Moscow?' asks Billy. 'The shooter, I mean, not the model.'

'Unlikely, given that the SVR have an entire directorate trained in assassination. And why would they have him killed in London when they could do it any time they wanted to at home?'

'Make a splash?' Billy shrugs. 'Show that no one's beyond their reach?'

'Possible, but our information is that the Kremlin were quite happy to tolerate Viktor and his far-right associates; they made the official regime look almost moderate. And they didn't hesitate to use his death against us. They've demanded a full investigation and made it clear, at diplomatic level, that they expect the killer caught. That demand has filtered down via Richard Edwards to me. To us.'

Lance purses his lips. 'So who was responsible for Kedrin's protection when he was in London?'

Eve meets his gaze. 'Officially, me. I was the liaison officer between MI5 and the Metropolitan Police.'

Lance lets her answer hang in the air. Above the patter of the rain, Eve can hear the faint wheeze of Billy's breathing.

'You said there's a second reason we want this woman.'

'She killed Simon Mortimer, the officer you're replacing. And yes, I know what the official Service report says, because I helped draft it. What actually happened is that she cut his throat, to send a message to me.'

'Shit,' murmurs Billy. Reaching into the pocket of his combat pants, he finds an inhaler, and takes two deep puffs.

'She cut his throat,' says Lance flatly. 'To send you a message.'

'Yes. You heard me right. So you might want to think quite carefully before agreeing to join this team.'

Lance looks at her for a moment. 'Where exactly do you see us going with all this?'

'We have a lead. The name of an individual who might be on the payroll of the organisation that runs our target. It's a long shot, but it's all we've got. So we follow the money, and we follow the man, and maybe, just maybe, we get to our killer.'

'Any chance of borrowing some A4 surveillance people from Thames House?'

'None whatsoever. This is a closed-circle operation, and no whisper of it leaves this room. Nor will you make any further contact, social or otherwise, with any Security Services personnel, on either side of the river. If anyone checks your files, you're both on official secondment to Customs and Excise. And I repeat, this could be dangerous. All the indications are that our target is not only highly trained and well-resourced, but a narcissistic sociopath who kills for pleasure.'

'I'm assuming the money's shit,' Lance says.

'You both stay at present pay-grades, yes.'

The two men look at each other. Then, very slowly, Billy nods, Lance shrugs his shoulders, and for the first time since their arrival Eve senses a flicker of common purpose.

'So,' Billy says. 'This lead you mentioned.'

As Villanelle runs, she feels her body relax into the familiar rhythm. Her back and thighs are still sore from the previous afternoon's ju-jitsu session at the Club d'Arts Martiaux in Montparnasse, but by the time that she's completed the circuit of the lake and the Auteuil racecourse, the stiffness has vanished. On her way home, she picks up a takeaway sushi order from Comme des Poissons and a copy of the financial paper *Les Echos*.

Back at the flat she showers, runs a comb through her dark-blonde hair, and pulls on jeans, a T-shirt and a leather jacket. Sitting on her balcony, she eats the sushi with her fingers and works her way through *Les Echos*. By the time she's finished the last mouthful of tuna, she's scanned every page and processed the information she needs.

Looking out over the city, she checks her phone. But there's no text from Konstantin. No new target. Turning on the Grundig shortwave radio, as she is required to do at least twice a day between actions, Villanelle keys in a search code. As usual, it takes a moment or two to find the number station, which tends to skip from frequency to frequency. Today it's broadcasting at 6840 kHz. There's a faint crackle, followed by the first fifteen notes of a Russian folk song, whose name Villanelle once knew but has long forgotten. The music's electronically generated, with a thin, tinny sound that's at once sad and faintly sinister. The notes repeat for two minutes, and then a woman's voice, distant but precise, begins to recite a five-digit Russian number group.

This is the call-up code, identifying the individual for whom the message is intended, and the voice has repeated the numbers three times – '*Dva, pyat', devyat', sem', devyat'* . . .' Two, five, nine, seven, nine – before Villanelle realises that the call-up code is her own. The shock momentarily takes her breath away. A number station call-out entails immediate action. She's been checking in with the station for more than two years without ever hearing her number.

The call-up repeats for four minutes, then six electronic chimes announce the message. Again, this consists of five-digit groups, each voiced twice. Then the chimes again, the opening notes of the folk song, and the hiss of empty air. It takes Villanelle ten minutes to decrypt the message using the one-time pad that she keeps, along with a SIG Sauer P226 automatic and €10,000 in high-denomination notes, in a concealed safe. It reads:

17NORTHSTAR.

Re-locking the safe, Villanelle grabs a baseball cap and sunglasses and leaves the flat. Location seventeen is the heliport at Issy-les-Moulineaux. Taking the ring road as fast as the traffic allows, whipping from lane to lane in the silver-grey Roadster, she makes it in fifteen minutes flat. At the entry gate to the car park, two men in high-visibility vests are waiting. They look vaguely official, and as Villanelle slows to a halt one of them holds out a placard printed with the words North Star. When Villanelle nods he beckons her out of the Audi and takes her car keys, then the second man leads her up an unmarked side road to a rectangle of tarmac enclosed by warehouses. At its central point, an Airbus Hummingbird helicopter is waiting, rotors idly turning.

Villanelle climbs into the seat beside the pilot, straps herself in, and places a noise-reducing communications headset over her baseball cap. She is carrying no luggage, money, passport or identifying documents.

'OK?' asks the pilot, his eyes invisible behind mirrored sunglasses.

Villanelle gives him a thumbs-up, and the Hummingbird lifts off, hovers for a moment above the heliport, and swings eastwards. Below them, briefly, is the serpentine glitter of the Seine, and the crawl of traffic on the Périphérique. And then the city falls away and there's just the thrum of the engine. Only now does Villanelle have time to wonder why she's been called out via the number station. And why there's been no word from Konstantin.

It's late afternoon by the time they touch down at Annecy Mont Blanc airfield in south-eastern France, where a lone figure is waiting on the tarmac. Something about her severely cropped hair and over-tight suit tells Villanelle that the woman is Russian, and this is confirmed when she speaks, directing Villanelle towards a dusty Peugeot parked fifty metres away. The woman drives with brisk efficiency, making a fast half-circuit of the airfield before pulling up with a screech of brakes in a hangar beside a Learjet bearing the North Star insignia.

'Inside,' she orders, slamming the car door, and Villanelle climbs the steps into the Learjet's climate-controlled interior and straps herself into a seat upholstered in arctic-blue leather. Following her, the woman retracts the steps and seals the exit door. The engines start immediately. There's a flare of late-afternoon sunshine at the window as the jet exits the hangar, and then, with a muted roar, they're airborne.

'So where are we going?' Villanelle enquires, releasing her seat-belt buckle.

The woman meets her gaze. She's got broad, high-cheekboned features and eyes the colour of slate. Something about her is familiar.

'East,' she says, snapping open an overnight bag at her feet. 'I've got your documents.'

A passport, Ukrainian, in the name of Angelika Pyatachenko. A worn leather wallet containing a driving licence, credit cards, and a reception pass identifying her as an employee of the North Star corporation. Crumpled receipts. A wad of rouble notes.

'And clothes. Please change now.'

A leather-look jacket, limp angora sweater, and short skirt. Scuffed ankle boots. Underwear, much washed. Cheap tights, new, from a Kiev department store.

Conscious that she's being scrutinised, Villanelle takes off her cap and sunglasses and begins to undress, laying her clothes on the blue leather seat. When she removes her bra, the other woman gasps.

'Shit. It really is you. Oxana Vorontsova.'

'I'm sorry?'

'I wasn't sure to begin with, but . . .'

Villanelle stares at her blankly. Konstantin promised her that the cut-out was total. That nothing like this could ever happen.

'What are you talking about?'

'You don't remember me? Lara? From Ekaterinburg?'

Fuck, it *can't* be. But it is. That girl from the military academy. She's cut her hair off, and looks older, but it's her. With a supreme effort of will, Villanelle keeps her face expressionless. 'Who do you think I am?'

'Oxana, I know who you are. You look different, but it's you. I thought I recognised that little scar on your mouth, and I knew for sure when I saw that mole on your breast. Don't you remember me?'

Villanelle considers the situation. Denial isn't going to work. 'Lara,' she says. 'Lara Farmanyants.'

They met, just a few years earlier, at the university games, when they were competing in the pistol-shooting. It had become clear that Farmanyants, representing the Kazan Military Academy, was going to be very hard to beat, so the night before the final Oxana slipped into her rival's room, and without speaking a word, stripped naked and climbed into bed with her. It didn't take the young cadet long to recover from her surprise. She was, as Oxana had guessed, badly in need of sex, and returned her kisses with the desperation of a starved animal. Later that night, dopey from hours of fervent cunnilingus, she whispered to Oxana that she loved her.

That was the moment when Oxana knew that she had won. Early the next morning she crept back to her own room, and when she saw Lara at breakfast in the canteen looked straight through her. Lara tried to approach her several times that morning, and each time Oxana blanked her. When they lined up at the target range, Lara's broad features registered hurt and bafflement. She tried to compose herself for the competition, but her aim wavered, and the best she could manage was a bronze medal. Oxana, shooting straight and true, took gold, and by the time she climbed onto the team coach to return to Perm, Lara Farmanyants had been deleted from her thoughts.

And now, by some malign coincidence, here she is again. Perhaps it isn't so strange that she should be working for Konstantin. She's a superb shot, and probably far too smart and ambitious to waste her career in the military.

'I read in the paper that you killed some Mafia people,' Lara says. 'And later, one of the instructors at the academy told me that you hanged yourself in prison. I'm glad that part wasn't true.'

Conscious that she needs to keep Lara onside, Villanelle softens her gaze. 'I'm sorry I treated you the way I did at Ekaterinburg.'

'You did what you had to do to win. And although it probably meant nothing to you, I've never forgotten that night.'

'Really?'

'Really and truly.'

'So how long is this flight?' Villanelle asks.

'Perhaps another two hours.'

'And will we be interrupted?'

'The pilot has instructions not to leave the cabin.'

'In that case . . .' She reaches out and runs a finger softly down Lara's cheek.

The light is fading when the Learjet touches down at a small private airfield outside Scherbanka in South Ukraine. A cold wind scours the runway, where a BMW high-security vehicle is waiting. Lara drives fast, leaving the airfield by a side-gate, where a uniformed guard waves them through. Their destination, she tells Villanelle, is Odessa. For an hour they proceed smoothly through the darkening landscape, but as they approach the city, they run into traffic. Ahead of them, illuminated by the lights of the city, the clouds are a sulphurous yellow.

'I won't say anything about you,' says Lara.

Villanelle inclines her head against the window. The first spatters of rain streak the armour-plated glass. 'It won't go well for you if you do. Oxana Vorontsova is dead.'

'A pity. I admired her.'

'You need to forget her.'

I'll speak to Konstantin, Villanelle decides. He can deal with Lara. Preferably with a 9mm round to the back of that neatly cropped head.

On her return from China, with the help of an investigator borrowed from the City of London's Economic Crime department, Eve attempted to chase down the lead Jin Qiang had given her: to identify who had made the bank transfer of £17 million, and who had been the beneficiary. The investigation failed to reveal the source of the funds, but led them via an intricate web of shell companies to the payee, a low-profile venture capitalist named Tony Kent.

Detailed investigation of Kent and his affairs revealed little, but one fact caught Eve's interest: that Kent was a member of an exclusive fly-fishing syndicate that owned half a mile of the River Itchen in Hampshire. Information about the syndicate was not easy to come by, but Richard Edwards was able, after a few discreet enquiries, to furnish Eve with a membership list. This was not long; indeed, it contained only six names. Those of Tony Kent, two hedge-fund managers, a partner in a high-profile commodity trading firm, a senior cardio-thoracic surgeon, and Dennis Cradle. Eve knew exactly who Dennis Cradle was. He was the director of D4 Branch at MI5, responsible for counter-espionage against Russia and China.

Billy is crouched at the steel desk that used to be Simon's, hacking into Dennis Cradle's email account. The new computer hardware, now connected and running, gives off a faint hum. Lance is sitting on a plastic chair in front of the window, staring at the traffic on Tottenham Court

Road. His contribution to the office decor has been a clothes rail, hung with coats and jackets that look like a job lot from a charity shop. In the teeth of all her principles, Eve has given him permission to smoke, as the pungent tang of his roll-ups masks other, worse odours.

'Did you have curry last night, Billy?' she asks, looking up from her laptop screen.

'Yeah, prawn Madras.' He shifts his buttocks in his chair. 'How d'you know?'

'Call it an inspired guess. How are you getting on with that password?'

'Nearly there, I think.' His fingers dance over the keyboard as he stares at his screen. 'Oh! You silly, silly man.'

'You in?' asks Lance.

'All the way. Dennis Cradle, you're my bitch.'

'So what've we got?' Eve asks, a tiny flame of excitement flaring inside her.

'Cloud server data. Everything on his home computer, basically.'

'Doesn't sound as if it's very secure.'

Billy shrugs. 'He probably thinks that because it's domestic stuff, he doesn't need heavy-duty authentication.'

'Or perhaps he doesn't want to give the impression of having anything to hide. Perhaps this is what we're supposed to see.'

Cradle shares an account with his wife, Penny, a corporate lawyer. Their emails are stored in orderly folders with names like Accounts, Cars, Health, Insurance and Schools. The inbox holds fewer than a hundred messages, which Billy copies and sends to Eve. A preliminary examination reveals little of interest.

'This is like a lifestyle advertisement,' says Eve, scrolling through the Cradles' picture files. Almost all of the images are of family activity holidays. Skiing in Megève, tennis camp in Malaga, sailing on the Algarve. Cradle himself is a tanned, bullish figure of about fifty, who clearly enjoys being photographed in sports kit. His wife, prettyish and well groomed, is perhaps five years younger. Their children, Daniel and Bella, stare at the camera with the sulky entitlement of privately schooled teenagers.

'Twats,' says Billy.

'Have a look at their London place,' says Eve.

The street-view image shows a red-brick Georgian house, set back from the road. A pillared porch is half-obscured by a spreading magnolia. A burglar alarm is visible beside a ground-floor window.

'Where is it?' asks Lance.

'Muswell Hill. They've been there six years. Cost them one point three mill. Today, it's got to be worth two, at least.'

'Surely Cradle's not pretending to have paid for all this on his Service salary?'

'No. The wife's the big earner.'

'Even so, they'll have trouble explaining away seventeen fat ones.'

Eve shrugs. 'I doubt they'll have to. Assuming that Tony Kent is acting as some sort of financial intermediary for the organisation we're targeting, I'd guess that money's parked well out of sight of the Revenue.'

'So how do we know it's going to Cradle?'

'We don't, for certain. But Jin Qiang wouldn't have directed me to Kent if he didn't know I'd make the connection with Cradle. I'd asked specific questions about the possibility that members of the UK Intelligence Services were receiving large-scale payments from any unknown source. This was Jin's answer. I think it was as far as he thought he could go.'

'So,' says Lance, 'are we going to turn Cradle's place over?'

Eve polishes her glasses. 'I'd like to, but it'll be well secured. He's a senior MI5 officer. The shit would really fly if we were caught.'

'I'm assuming we're not going the search warrant route?'

'No. We'd never get one, even if we said why we needed one. Which we can't.'

'Just asking.' Lance leans in towards the screen. 'That's a dummy alarm beside the window, so they've probably got a conventional system inside. Infra-red, pressure pads . . .'

'You think it's doable?' Eve asks him.

He flicks his lighter beneath his half-smoked roll-up. 'Everything's doable. It's a question of opportunity. Can you get the bloke's diary up, Billy?'

'I've got Penny's. He doesn't seem to have one.'

'I need a guaranteed two-hour window. What can they offer us?'

'How about this?' says Billy. 'Dinner with A & L, Mazeppa 8.00.'

Eve frowns. 'But that's tonight.'

'I can do tonight.' Lance shrugs. 'I'll cancel my date with Gigi Hadid.'

'Too soon. We need to do a proper recce. We can't just go charging in there. What else have they got coming up?'

'Don't know about Dennis,' says Billy. 'But Penny's not got anything else booked this week.'

'Fuck.' Eve searches for Mazeppa on her phone. It's a Michelin-starred restaurant in Dover Street, Mayfair. She looks uncertainly at Lance.

'I could check the house out this afternoon,' he offers. 'Park up and sit tight. Soon as they leave this evening, in we go.'

Eve nods. It's far from ideal. And she has no idea about Lance's skills as a housebreaker. But Richard wouldn't have sent her a dud operative. And she needs results.

'OK,' she says.

Lara has dropped Villanelle off at a cafe in Odessa's Bird Market, in the Moldovanka district. It's a dingy place, with yellowish lighting, faded travel posters on the walls, and a blackboard advertising the day's special. Perhaps half of the tables are occupied. By single men, mostly, and a couple of women who might be prostitutes, fuelling themselves for the night's work with *solyanka* soup and dumplings. From time to time the men glance at Villanelle, but on meeting her flatly hostile gaze, look away again.

She's been waiting here for twenty minutes now, sipping a cup of tea and skim-reading a copy of *Sevodnya*, a Russian-language tabloid, in one of the booths at the side of the room. At intervals she raises her eyes to the cafe's rain-blurred glass frontage, and the dimly lit streets beyond. She's hungry, but doesn't order anything in case she has to leave.

A lean figure slips into the booth opposite her. A man she's met before: the man who talked to her in Hyde Park the previous winter, and who spooked her.

And now here he is again. There are the patchy beginnings of a beard, and a battered leather jacket has replaced the tailored coat, but the frozen darkness of the eyes is the same.

When they first met he spoke English, but now he is calling to the elderly waitress in fluent, Moscow-accented Russian.

'You're hungry?' he asks, running a hand through rain-damp hair.

She shrugs.

'*Borscht* and *pirozhki* for two,' he orders, and sits back.

'So,' says Villanelle, her face expressionless.

'So we meet again.' He gives her the ghost of a smile. 'I apologise for failing to identify myself in London. The time wasn't right.'

'And now it is?'

He looks at her, assessingly. 'We were impressed by your handling of the Kedrin action. And now we are faced with a situation requiring your assistance.'

'I see.'

'You don't see, but you will. My name is Anton, and I'm a colleague of the man you know as Konstantin.'

'Go on.'

'Konstantin has been abducted. Taken hostage by a mafia gang, based here in Odessa.'

She stares at him, speechless.

'And yes, we're quite sure. The gang is called *Zoloty Bratstvo*, or the Golden Brotherhood, and it's headed by a man named Rinat Yevtukh. According to our information, Konstantin is being held in a well-secured house in Fontanka, a half-hour away from here. The house is owned by Yevtukh. The gang's intention, apparently, is to demand a ransom.'

Her expression remains neutral, but alarm is jolting through her with nauseating force. Is this a set-up? An attempt to panic her into revealing who and what she is?

'You have to trust me,' he says. 'If I was a hostile, you'd be dead already.'

Still she says nothing. Even if he's telling the truth, and Konstantin has been abducted, she's still lethally compromised. If they – whoever 'they' are – can get to Konstantin, with his serpentine wariness, then they can get to her.

'Tell me,' she says eventually.

'OK. We're certain that the kidnappers know nothing about Konstantin's connection to us, or even that we exist. As far as they're are concerned, he's just a visiting businessman, whose company will pay up in the usual way. What concerns us is that Yevtukh's organisation has, for some time, been under the control of the SVR, the Russian secret intelligence service. And the SVR have wind of us, as MI6 do. They don't know who or what we are, but they know we exist. So the question is, have they organised this abduction with a view to interrogating Konstantin about us? We're not sure. We've got our own people in the SVR, naturally, but it'll take time to find out what's really going on. And we don't have time.'

He pauses as bowls, spoons and a steaming casserole of *borscht* are placed on their table, followed moments later by a plate of *pirozhki* – small buns filled with minced meat. As the waitress shuffles away, Anton ladles out the beetroot soup, splashing the front of Villanelle's cheap sweater with spots of dark purple.

'Konstantin's tough,' he continues. 'But even he can't beat an SVR interrogation.'

Villanelle nods, dabbing absently at her sweater with a paper napkin. 'So what do you propose?'

'We get him out.'

'We?'

'Yes. I've assembled a team of our best people.'

She meets his gaze. 'I don't work with other people.'

'You do now.'

'I'll be the one who decides that.'

He leans in towards her. 'Listen, we don't have time for this primadonna shit. You'll do what you're told. And there's a good chance we can all walk away from this.'

She sits there, motionless. 'I've never taken part in a hostage-rescue.'

'Just listen, OK. You have a very specific role to play.'

She listens. And knows that she has no choice. That all that she is, all that she has become, hangs on the success of this mission.

'I'll do it on one condition. That I'm not recognisable. I don't want anyone else on the team to see my face. Or find out anything about me.'

'Don't worry, the others feel the same. You'll wear full-face masks throughout, and communication will be limited to an operational minimum. Afterwards, when the mission's completed, you'll be returned separately to where you came from.'

She nods. There's so much about him that she distrusts, and from which she instinctively recoils. But she can't, at that moment, find fault with his plan.

'So when do we go in?'

He surveys the cafe, and takes a mouthful of soup. The rain beats harder against the glass frontage.

'Tonight.'

Niko doesn't raise his voice, but Eve can hear that he's upset. Two of his colleagues from the school are expected for dinner, Chilean Pinot Noir has been bought, and a small but expensive shoulder of lamb is waiting in an oven-proof dish, stuck with cloves of garlic. The subtext to the evening is that Eve will make herself look nice, and wear the St Laurent scent he bought her, and her prettiest earrings, and when the guests have gone they will make slightly drunken love, and things will, one way and another, be OK again.

'I can't believe that it – whatever *it* is – really has to happen tonight,' he says. 'I mean, Jesus, Eve. Seriously. You've known about Zbig and Claudia coming over for weeks.'

'I'm sorry,' she says, conscious of Billy listening to every word. 'I just can't do tonight. Nor can I discuss this on an open line. You'll just have to apologise for me.'

'So what am I going to say? That you're working late? I thought all that finished when you . . .'

'Niko, please. Tell them whatever you like. You know the situation.'

'No I don't, actually, Eve. I really don't. I have a life, in case you haven't noticed, and I'm asking you, just this once, to do something for me. So make an excuse, do whatever you have to, but be there this evening. If you're not . . .'

'Niko, I—'

'No, listen to me. If you're not, then we need to think very seriously about whether—'

'Niko, it's an emergency. There's a threat to life, and I've been ordered to stay.'

Silence, except for the rise and fall of his breathing.

'I'm sorry, I have to go.'

As she breaks the connection Eve catches Billy's eye, and he looks away. She stands there for a moment, dizzy with shame. This is not the first time that she's avoided the truth with Niko, but it's the first time that she's straight out lied to him.

And for what? Billy and Lance could handle this just fine without her. In fact they'd probably prefer to, but something deep inside her, something savage and atavistic, wants to run with the pack. Is it worth it? Turning her life into this furtive twilight, and testing the love of a good man to destruction? Is she onto something with Dennis Cradle, or just forging imaginary links to deceive herself she's making progress?

If they find nothing on Cradle, she'll take time off. Make things right with Niko, if it's not too late. All the longer-serving officers at Thames House said the same thing: you had to have a life outside. If you didn't want to end up alone, you had to tear yourself away from the sleepless intoxication of secret work. All it offered was an unending series of false horizons. And no closure, ever.

Thinking of Niko at home without her, laying the table, setting out the wine glasses, carefully placing the lamb in the oven, makes her want to weep. The temptation to ring him, to say that the situation's resolved and that she's coming straight home, is overwhelming. But she doesn't.

'Have you got a girlfriend, Billy?'

'Not as such. Chat with this girl on Sea of Souls.'

'What's Sea of Souls?'

'Online role-player game.'

'So what's she called?'

'Her user name's Ladyfang.'

'Ever met her?'

'Nah. Was thinking about pushing for a date, but she'd probably turn out to be really old, or a bloke, or something.'

'That's a bit sad, isn't it?'

Billy shrugs. 'To be honest I haven't got time for a girl-friend right now.' There's a brief silence, broken by the buzz of his phone. 'It's Lance. He's parked up, with eyes on the house. No sign of any occupants.'

'They won't be back from work yet. And my guess is that they'll both go straight to the restaurant. He'll be coming from Thames House. Her firm's based out at Canary Wharf. But we can't count on it. Our clock starts at eight, when they meet the others at Mazeppa.'

'I'll ring my mum. Tell her not to wait up.'

The forward operating base is a disused farmhouse two miles north-west of Fontanka. The assault team is gathered in a rectangular outbuilding housing a rusting ZAZ hatchback and an assortment of mud-caked agricultural implements. Temporary spotlights illuminate two long trestle tables bearing maps, architectural plans and a laptop computer. Metal boxes containing weaponry, ammunition and equipment are stacked on the earth floor. It's 10 p.m., local time. Beyond the farmyard wall, silhouetted against the darkening sky, Villanelle can see the rotors of a Little Bird military helicopter.

In addition to Anton, the team numbers five. Four assaulters, of whom Villanelle is one, and a sniper. All five are wearing black Nomex coveralls, body armour, and close-fitting balaclava masks. Villanelle has no idea of the identity of the others, but Anton is conducting the final briefing in English.

The building in which Konstantin is being held, they learn, stands in grounds of half-a-dozen acres. Photographs show an ostentatious three-storey palazzo with pillars, balustrades and a steeply pitched tile roof. A chain-link fence surrounds the estate; entry is by means of a guarded electronic gate. To Villanelle, the place looks like a fortified wedding cake.

The assaulters can expect a fight. According to intelligence gained by surveillance, there's a permanent armed security detail of six men attached to the house, of whom up to three, at any one time, are patrolling the exterior. Given Yevtukh's reputation, and the probability that most are ex-military, they're likely to mount a strong resistance.

Anton's plan is simple: a surgical strike of such savagery and intensity as to leave the hostage-takers incapable of coordinated response. As the assault team clears the house, the sniper will seek targets of opportunity. Speed will be of the essence.

Villanelle looks around her at the other masked figures. The Nomex suits and body armour give them all the same bulky profile, but the sniper has the body-mass of a woman. They will be known to each other only by their call signs. The assaulters are Alpha, Bravo, Charlie and Delta, the sniper is Echo.

With the tactical briefing completed, the assaulters move to the weaponry boxes. After some thought, Villanelle arms herself with a KRISS Vector sub-machine gun, a Glock 21 handgun, several magazines loaded with .45 ACP rounds, and a Gerber combat knife. Then from one of the trestle tables she takes a fibre-optic scope and viewer, and the helmet carry-bag marked with her call sign, Charlie. Slipping the scope into a thigh pocket, she takes the helmet outside into the darkened farmyard to check the intercom and night-vision goggles. Around her there are brief illuminations as the other three assaulters test weapon-mounted torches and laser sights.

Lifting off the ballistic helmet, she watches them. There's a tall guy, Delta, with dark-skinned hands, who's shouldering a heavy combat shotgun. Bravo is a wiry figure of medium height, wholly anonymous, and Alpha is bullish and compact. Both are carrying short-barrelled Heckler & Koch sub-machine guns and multiple bandoliers of ammunition. All three are, without question, male, and she's aware of them checking her out in return, eyes expressionless behind their face masks. Half-a-dozen paces away the sniper, armed with a Lobaev SVL rifle and night-scope, is measuring crosswind vectors with a velocity meter.

Inside the farmhouse the team finalises communications and radio procedure. The voices of the others are unrevealing; all speak fluent English, although with differing accents. Alpha sounds Eastern European, Bravo is definitely southern-states American, and Delta's first language is probably Arabic. Echo, the woman, is Russian. And to these faceless creatures, Villanelle muses, I have to entrust my life. Fucking hell.

Smoothing out the maps and architectural plans, Anton beckons to them.

'OK. Last run-through, then we go. I'd have liked to hit the house some time before dawn tomorrow morning, but we can't risk leaving the hostage there that long. So listen in.'

As he speaks, Villanelle is aware of the sniper, Echo, standing beside her. Their eyes meet, and she recognises the slate-grey gaze of Lara Farmanyants.

Yet again, Villanelle feels her bearings shift. Lara naked and supine beneath her is one thing, Lara hefting a high-precision rifle quite another. Is she there merely to take out the guards, or is she part of some unfathomably devious plan of Anton's?

192

The two women regard each other for a moment, expressionless.

'Nice weapon,' Villanelle says.

'It's my favourite for this kind of work. Chambered for .408 Chey-Tac.' Lara works the Lobaev's soundlessly smooth bolt action. 'I'm not so easily distracted from my aim, these days.'

'I'm sure you're not. Good hunting.'

Lara nods, and a minute later climbs into the SUV which will take her to her firing position.

The minutes creep past. Villanelle fits the ear cups of her helmet, adjusts her microphone boom, and tightens her chinstrap. Finally, a signal from Echo informs Anton that she is in position and ready. Anton nods at the four assaulters and they make their way through the darkened farmyard to the matt-black Little Bird. The pilot is waiting in the unlit cockpit, and readies the craft for take-off as the assaulters take their places on the outboard fuselage platforms. Seating herself on the starboard platform, with the KRISS Vector slung across her chest, Villanelle clips on the retaining harness. Next to her, Delta is holding the shotgun across his knees. His eyes narrow, and they exchange wary nods.

There's a muted roar as the Little Bird's engine engages, followed by the accelerating *whump-whump* of the rotors. The craft shudders, Delta extends a gloved arm, and he and Villanelle bump fists. For now, whatever the future might hold, they're a team, and Villanelle forces her apprehensions to the back of her mind. The Little Bird lifts a few metres and hovers. Then the ground falls away as they climb into the night sky.

The helicopter approaches the villa upwind, then angles in fast, skimming over the chain-link fence before dancing in the air a metre above the lawn to the east of the main entrance. Releasing their harnesses the assaulters jump down, weapons levelled, and seconds later the Little Bird lifts and swings away into the darkness.

As they sprint for the cover of the side of the house, high-intensity security floodlights bathe the area in dazzling white. Two figures race towards them across the driveway. There's a wet smack, then another, and both go down on the gravel. One writhes like a pinned insect, and the other lies still, all but decapitated by the silenced .408 sniper round.

'Nice shooting, Echo,' murmurs Bravo, his Southern drawl pin-sharp in Villanelle's earphones, and with a series of aimed shots, begins to knock out the LED floodlights mounted on the lawn and the front of the building. Alpha runs to the rear corner of the building to perform the same operation there. Villanelle watches and waits. Muted by her helmet's noise-suppression system, the shots sound distant and unreal.

With only the far wall of the house still spotlit, the western portion of the grounds is thrown into sharp relief. Villanelle risks a quick glance round the angle of the building and feels the air ripple as a round passes her face. The shooter must have betrayed his position because Villanelle hears, once again, the meaty thwack of a sniper round finding its target. In her headphones, Lara's voice is calm. 'Echo to all players, you are now clear to breach. Repeat, you are clear to breach.'

What follows is a study in time and motion. Alpha runs out to the large central front door, places shaped explosive charges against it, and rejoins the others. The front door blows with a deafening *whoomph*, but this is a diversion. The real assault is through a small side door, which Delta

194

blows off its hinges with his shotgun. The assaulters pour through, into the deserted kitchens.

There's a formal choreography to house clearance. It's a self-propelling process that cannot and must not be halted. The team moves from room to room, with each member assigned a quadrant, sweeping, clearing, moving on. Villanelle knows the dance well, has rehearsed every step in the killing house at Delta Force's training facility at Fort Bragg. The instructors there knew her as Sylvie Dazat, on secondment from the GIGN, France's National Gendarmerie Intervention Group, and in her final assessment described her as an exceptionally fast learner with instinctive weapon skills, but with a personality so antisocial as to rule her out of any teamwork role. Her hostile behaviour had been deliberate. Men make themselves forget women who are unimpressed by them; Konstantin had taught her that. And no one at Fort Bragg remembers Sylvie Dazat.

They're in an anteroom now, full of overstuffed furniture. On the wall is a vast painting of Michael Jackson fondling a chimpanzee. From somewhere in the interior of the building comes the muffled thump of feet on stairs. A security guard edges into view levelling an assault rifle, and Villanelle spins him to his knees with a three-round burst from the KRISS Vector. He balances for a moment, blank-eyed, and falls face down. As she fires a double tap through the back of his skull, spattering the deep-pile carpet with blood, Bravo throws a stun grenade through the doorway towards the main body of the house.

A tidal wave of sound rolls over Villanelle, punching through her helmet, and Alpha and Bravo race past her. As she and Delta follow, leaping over the body of the guard, her ears sing. They're in an oversized hallway, which is hung with a pall of oily smoke from the stun grenade. For a couple of seconds the place appears unoccupied, then there's a fusillade of automatic-weapon fire, and the assaulters dive for cover.

Villanelle and Delta are crouching behind a large Chesterfield sofa upholstered in turquoise calfskin. Behind them is the main entrance, now open to the night, with the heavy front door sagging on its hinges. To their left, on a marble plinth, is a life-size statue of a ballerina naked except for a thong. A burst of fire rakes the sofa, tearing into the scatter cushions. If we stay here, Villanelle thinks, we're dead. And I really, really don't want to die here, among these criminally ugly furnishings.

Delta points at a gilt-framed mirror reflecting the far end of the hall. In it, a figure is just visible behind a large, ornate desk. As one, Villanelle and Delta rise from each end of the sofa. As she gives covering fire, he blasts the desk with the shotgun. Wood chips fly, and a body pitches heavily to the floor. Four down. There's a movement in the opposite corner, and a rifle barrel shows above a white leather armchair. Bravo smacks a burst into the upholstery, and a mist of blood reddens the zebra-print wallpaper. Five.

Ducking back behind the sofa, Villanelle changes magazines and runs for the stairs. The remaining hostage-taker, she guesses, is waiting on the first floor.

She inches up the stairs, and cautiously brings her eyes level with the first floor. A figure appears in the nearest doorway, she fires, and her head is whipped back with such force that, for a moment, she's certain that she's been shot. She falls to a crouch, her ears ringing, and is steadied by a hand to her shoulder. Pinpoints of light are bursting in front of her eyes.

'OK?' a familiar voice asks.

Villanelle nods, too dazed to wonder why Lara's there, and reaches a hand to her helmet. There's a deep furrow scored through the armoured plastic; a centimetre lower and it would have been her skull.

'You both fired at the same time,' Lara says. 'And luckily for you, he fired high.'

The sixth guard is lying on his back in the doorway. The ragged, sucking sound of his breath indicates a lung shot. With Villanelle covering her, Lara runs up to him, an automatic in her right hand.

'Where's the hostage?' she asks in Russian.

The guard looks upwards.

'Next floor up?'

The faintest of nods.

'Anyone guarding him?'

The eyes flutter and close.

'No one?'

The reply is an indistinguishable mumble. Lara leans closer, but all she can hear is the sucking of his chest. Levelling the handgun, she fires a single round between his eyes.

'What are you doing here?' Villanelle says.

'The same as you.'

'That wasn't the plan.'

'The plan has changed. I'm your back-up.'

Villanelle hesitates for a moment, and then biting back her doubts, leads Lara up the last few stairs. At the top, facing her, is a door. Taking out the fibre-optic scope, Villanelle slips the flexible 1mm cable over the carpet and under the door. The tiny fish-eye lens shows a brightly lit room, empty except for a figure trussed to a chair.

Silently, Villanelle tries the door. It's locked. A single round from the KRISS Vector blows out the cylinder, she kicks it open, and she and Lara burst into the room.

Together, they attend to the figure on the chair. There's a black cloth bag over his head, stiff with dried blood. Underneath it, Konstantin's face is battered. He has been gagged, and his breathing rattles through a broken nose.

As Lara removes the gag, Villanelle draws her combat knife and severs the PlastiCuffs binding Konstantin to the chair. He slumps to one side, his bruised and bloodied head thrown back, working his swollen fingers and drawing air into his lungs.

'I know what you're thinking,' Lara tells Villanelle. 'You're thinking that you'll never be safe as long as I'm alive, because I know who you really are. You're thinking about killing me.'

'This would be the perfect moment,' agrees Villanelle.

'You can also see how that puts me in the same position. How I'll never be safe as long as *you're* alive.'

'True again.'

'Oxana? Lara?' Konstantin whispers through lips dark with dried blood. 'It's you, isn't it?'

Both women turn to him. Neither removes her balaclava.

'I never told them anything. You know that, don't you?'

'I know that,' says Villanelle. She glances at Lara, notes the deceptive casualness of her stance, and the tautness of her index finger on the trigger guard of the automatic.

Konstantin's eyes move to Lara. 'I heard what you said. You two have no cause to fear each other.'

Lara's gaze narrows, but she doesn't speak.

Villanelle genuflects, so that her face is level with Konstantin's, and her body shielded from Lara by his. Reaching behind her back, she draws the Glock from its holster.

'Something you once told me,' she says to Konstantin. 'I've never forgotten it.'

'What was that?'

'Trust no one,' she says, and placing the barrel of the Glock against his ribs, squeezes the trigger.

Gaining entry to the Cradles' house is something of an anticlimax. After disabling the burglar alarm with a signal-jammer, Lance lets himself and Billy in through the front door with a set of skeleton keys. Helpfully, the Cradles have left their lights on, to discourage intruders.

Eve drives away, doubles round the block, and pulls up beneath a street light fifty metres away. In the shadowed passenger seat she's almost invisible, but she can see pedestrians and traffic coming from both directions. She knows what the Cradles look like. She's seen Dennis often enough at Thames House, and Penny at a couple of the rather grim drinks parties that the Service feels moved to organise each December. She's confident that she'll recognise them.

She's instructed Lance and Billy to go straight to the study and concentrate on the computers. To download everything on every drive that they can find, and copy any documents that they think might be relevant with handheld laser scanners. Both men seem to be experienced burglars; presumably this was what Richard Edwards meant when he described them as 'enterprising'.

Eve sits in the car, her mood switching between acute anxiety and boredom. After what seems like a dangerously lengthy interlude, she sees Billy sauntering along the pavement towards her.

'We're pretty much done,' he says, subsiding into the passenger seat. 'Lance wonders if you'd like to take a quick shufti.'

Confidence, Eve tells herself. Look respectable, press the bell, march in through the front door. Lance lets her in and hands her a pair of surgical gloves. The front hall is narrow, with a tiled floor and white gloss woodwork. There's a sitting room to the left, and a kitchen beyond the staircase. Eve feels her heart pounding. There's something profoundly shocking about trespassing in this way. 'Fancy some toast and Earl Grey?' Lance asks.

'Don't joke, I'm starving,' says Eve, steadying her voice. 'What've we got?'

'This way.'

Dennis Cradle's office is a neat, rather smug little room, with built-in shelving and bookcases, a desk in the same pale wood, and an ergonomic office chair. On the desktop is a powerful-looking computer with a twenty-four-inch monitor.

'Assuming Billy's gutted that,' Eve says.

'If it's on there, we've got it. Plus an external drive and various memory sticks we found in the drawers.'

'Is there a safe?'

'Not in here. There might be one somewhere else in the house, but even if we found one, I doubt we'd have time to crack it before they get back.'

Eve shakes her head. 'No, if there's anything we need, it'll be in here. I very much doubt he'd share the kind of information we're looking for with his wife.'

'Sensible bloke,' murmurs Lance.

Eve ignores him. 'So looking round here, what do you see?'

'Controlling type. And pretty pleased with himself, I'd say.'

The photos, mounted in a group on the wall above the desk, show Cradle with friends in a university dining hall, shaking hands with a US Army general, catching a salmon in a mountainous river, and posing with his family on holiday. The shelves hold a mix of bestselling thrillers, political memoirs, and titles related to security and Intelligence issues.

Lance's phone buzzes. 'It's Billy. The Cradles are outside. Getting out of a taxi. Time to go.'

'Shit. *Shit*.'

Lance moves fast and silently. Eve follows, her heart pounding so hard she thinks she's going to vomit. In the kitchen Lance slips the garden door latch, hurries Eve out, and quietly closes the door behind them. They're on soft ground now, some kind of lawn. *Shit*. Why are the Cradles back so early?

'Into the lane,' Lance orders. Overhung by bushes, this leads to the road. Eve swings a leg awkwardly over the low fence, thorns tearing at her clothes. Desperately, she wrenches herself free, and Lance follows her.

'OK, lie down.' He presses a hand between her shoulder blades. The ground is hard, uneven and wet.

'The lights,' she hisses, struggling to control her breathing. 'We left the fucking lights on.'

'They were on when we went in. Chill.'

Angry noises issue from the Cradles' kitchen. A banging of cupboard doors. Utensils slammed onto hard surfaces.

'When I say the word, make for the road,' whispers Lance.

'What are we waiting for?'

'Dennis. He's still in front, paying the taxi driver.'

Eve wills Penny to stay in the kitchen. She doesn't. Eve hears the garden door pushed open, and a thumb flicking at a cigarette lighter. Moments later, she smells smoke. Penny can't be more than a couple of metres away. Rigid with the fear of discovery, Eve barely dares to breathe.

There's the faint sound of the closing front door, and of a male voice. Eve presses herself even harder into the ground. Her face is inches from Lance's shoe.

'Look, I'm sorry, OK.' The man's voice, much closer now. 'But I honestly don't see . . .'

'You don't see? Well for a start, you condescending *shit*, you don't *ever* tell me to calm down in front of our friends.'

'Penny, please. Don't shout.'

'I'll shout as loud as I fucking well like.'

'Fine, but not in the garden, OK? We've got neighbours.'

'Fuck the neighbours.' Her voice drops. 'And fuck you, too.'

A brief silence, then something flips over the fence, and lands in Eve's hair with a tiny scorching hiss. The kitchen door clicks shut, and Eve claws at the half-smoked cigarette, melting the latex glove and burning her fingers before she finally tears it loose.

'Go,' whispers Lance.

Wincing with pain, Eve follows him down the lane to the road. No one seems to be watching as they climb into the car, but she's glad they've got false number plates.

'What's that smell?' asks Billy, letting out the clutch.

'My hair,' says Eve, pulling off the half-melted glove.

'Crikey, I won't ask. I'm assuming we're all going back to Goodge Street?'

'Billy, we don't have to go through all this stuff tonight,' Eve says.

'Maybe, but let's do it anyway. There's bugger-all on TV.'

'Lance?'

'Yeah, whatever.'

'Everyone good with pizza?' Billy asks. 'We passed a place on the Archway Road.'

It's nearly midnight when Eve rings Niko. He's at home, and the two other teachers who have come to dinner are still there.

'Niko, look, I'm really sorry about tonight, and I'll make it up to you, but I need to ask you something. Something important.'

Niko grunts non-committally.

'I need your help. Can you come to the office?'

'Now?'

'Yes, I'm afraid now.'

'Jesus, Eve.' He pauses. 'So what do I do with Zbig and Claudia?'

She considers. 'How good are they?'

'What do you mean, good?'

'IT stuff. Security protocols. Cracking.'

'They're very clever people. But right now, they're shit-faced.'

'You trust them?'

'Yeah, I trust them.' He sounds weary. Resigned.

'Niko, I'm sorry. I'll never ask you for anything again.'

'Yes, you will. Tell me.'

'Call a cab, and get over here. All of you.'

'Eve, you're forgetting. I don't know where "here" is. I don't know where anything is any more.'

'Niko . . .'

'Just tell me, OK?'

When she puts down the phone the others are looking at her. Billy's hands are poised, unmoving, above his keyboard. 'Are you sure this is a good idea?' Lance asks.

She meets his gaze. 'We've looked at everything on the external drive and the memory sticks, and everything we downloaded from his hard drive, and it's all squeaky-clean. We've just got this one locked file, and I'm afraid that if we don't crack it, everything else we did tonight counts for fuck all. Dennis Cradle is old-school MI5. He's not a techie, but he knows how to create a high-entropy password. Billy's brute force attack isn't working. We need more heads on this one, and I've got clearance from Richard to use outside consultants if necessary.'

'So who are these people?' Lance asks.

'My husband's Polish, and an ex-chess champion. He teaches maths, but he's a pretty damn good hacker. Zbigniew is his friend, a classics scholar, and Claudia is Zbig's girlfriend. She's an educational psychologist. They're smart people.'

'What about Official Secrets?'

'We're just asking them to help us crack a password. Nothing more. We're not going to name any names, give them context, or show them what we find in the file.'

Lance shrugs. 'OK by me, I guess.'

'Billy?'

'Yeah. What he said.'

'So would you have killed me?' Villanelle asks.

'Those were my orders,' says Lara. 'If you didn't finish Konstantin off, I was to shoot you, and then him. He was compromised.'

'He wouldn't have told them anything.'

'You know that, and I know that. But it's not theoretically impossible, so he had to die, and you had to kill him, and I was the back-up. That's how they operate, our employers.'

'You haven't answered my question. Would you have killed me?'

'Yes.'

They're lying, naked, on the Learjet's foldaway bed. They smell of sweat, sex and gunshot residue. In forty minutes they will land at Vnukovo airport, south-west of Moscow. Lara will leave, and Villanelle will continue to Paris via Annecy Mont Blanc and Issy-les-Moulineaux. There will be no official record of her entering France, just as there was no record of her leaving.

She strokes the nape of Lara's neck. Feels the prickle of her cropped hair. 'You were good tonight. That running head-shot was perfection.'

'Thank you.'

'You practically decapitated him.'

'I know. That Lobaev's a dream to shoot.' Gently, she takes Villanelle's upper lip between her teeth, and explores it with her tongue. 'I love your scar. How did you get it?'

'It doesn't matter.'

'I want to know,' says Lara, reaching between Villanelle's legs. 'Tell me.'

Villanelle begins to answer, but feeling the slippery flutter of Lara's fingers inside her, arches her back and sighs, her body's pulse becoming one with the engine-note of the Learjet. She pictures the aircraft racing through the night, and the dark Russian forests far below. Taking Lara's other hand in hers, she sucks the trigger finger into her mouth. It tastes metallic and sulphurous, like death.

Eve meets Niko and his friends outside Goodge Street tube station. Niko touches a hand to her arm, the gesture stiff and self-conscious, and she smells plum brandy on his breath. Zbig is wild and bear-like and visibly drunk, and Claudia is glacial and avoids Eve's eye. Looking at them, Eve feels her optimism fade.

In the office Lance has made tea, and noting Claudia's expression, has slipped outside for a roll-up. The temperature is dropping. Eve finds everyone chairs.

'So how can we help?' asks Claudia, her face expressionless, her hands taut at the collar of her coat.

Eve looks at the assembled faces. 'We have a password to break.'

Niko looks at Billy. 'Life or death, I understand.'

'You could say.'

'So what are you trying?'

'Right now, a series of dictionary attacks. If that doesn't do it, I'm going to try a rainbow table. But that'll take time.'

'Which we don't have,' says Eve.

Claudia frowns, still holding her collar tightly closed. 'How much do you know about the password-holder?'

'A bit.'

'You think we can possibly guess the password?'

'I think we can have a bloody good try.'

Claudia looks at Zbig, who shrugs, and blows the steam off his tea.

'Tell us about this guy,' says Niko.

'Smart, middle-aged, well educated . . .' Eve begins. 'Computer-literate, but not a full-on geek. He would have people to take care of issues like computer and network security at work. But the file we need to crack was hidden on his home computer, so probably password-locked by himself.'

'How well was it hidden?' asks Claudia.

'Billy?'

'Executable .bat file. Not completely entry-level.'

'My instinct about this guy,' Eve says, 'is that he would consider himself clever enough to create an uncrackable password. He'll have informed himself about things like information entropy . . .'

'Like what?' asks Zbig.

Niko rubs his eyes. 'Password strength is measured in entropy bits, which represent the base-2 logarithm of the number of guesses it would take to break it.'

Zbig stares. 'Sorry . . . *what*?'

'You don't need to know all that,' says Claudia. 'What Eve means is that our target is smart enough to know that the password will have to be obscure, it will have to be long, and it will have to incorporate different types of characters.'

'He's arrogant,' says Eve. 'It won't be something random. The password will mean something to him. Something he thinks no one will ever guess. And I'd put money on the fact that there's a clue in plain sight in his office, which is why Billy photographed everything on his desk, on the walls, and in the bookcase. We've just got to out-think him.'

Lance reappears, smelling of cigarettes, and Billy spreads out the A4 prints. There's a shot of the desktop, showing Cradle's computer, landline phone, anglepoise lamp, DAB radio and binoculars, as well as miniature busts of Mao Tse Tung and Lenin.

'Communist kitsch,' murmurs Niko. 'Dickhead.'

The shots of the books show copies of Shakespeare's *Hamlet*, Machiavelli's *The Prince* and Donald Trump's *Great Again*, political thrillers by John le Carré and Charles Cumming, memoirs by David Petraeus and Geri Halliwell, and two shelves of Intelligence-related titles.

Other photographs are of pictures on the study wall. The students in the university dining hall, Cradle shaking hands with the US four-star general, the salmon-fishing shots, and the family holiday snaps.

'Remember,' Eve says, as she refills the kettle for another round of tea. 'The word or phrase we're looking for could have as many as thirty characters. Think of quotes. Ex public-school types like Cradle love quotes; they're a way of showing off how well read they are.'

An hour passes, punctuated by speculative bursts of talk, flurries of key strokes, and the growl of night-traffic on the Tottenham Court Road. Lance goes outside for another roll-up. A second hour passes. Hangovers begin to bite, faces take on a defeated aspect, and Zbig mutters in Polish.

'What did he say?' Eve asks Niko.

'He said that this is about as much fun as fucking a hedgehog.'

'Right, well, let's take a break and see where we are.' She stands up and looks at the others. 'Can I have your best guesses so far? We've got three attempts at this password before the system locks down, so before we try one we need to be really sure we're in with a chance. Niko, do you want to go first?'

'OK. My best shot is something based on "Methinks it is like a weasel".'

'Don't get it,' says Eve.

'It's a quote,' says Niko. 'From *Hamlet*. There's a copy of *Hamlet* in the bookcase.'

'So?'

'The Weasel Program is also the name of a mathematical experiment by Richard Dawkins. It's based on the theory that, given enough time, a monkey hitting random characters on a typewriter could produce the complete works of Shakespeare. Dawkins says that even if you just take the phrase "Methinks it is like a weasel", and a keyboard limited to twenty-six letters and a space bar, it would still take a high-speed computer program longer than the life of the universe to generate the correct phrase, given that there are . . .'

'Twenty-seven to the power of twenty-eight possible combinations,' says Billy.

'Exactly.'

'Would our subject know about this Weasel thing?' asks Claudia.

'No reason why not,' says Eve. 'And *Hamlet* is definitely the odd one out in that bookcase. Anything else, Niko?'

He shakes his head.

'*Scream If You Wanna Go Faster*?' suggests Claudia.

'That's not from *Hamlet*,' says Zbig.

'Funny guy. No, it's Geri Halliwell's second album. I bought it when I was sixteen. I used to sing "It's Raining Men" into my hairbrush in front of the bathroom mirror.'

'Zbig?'

'How about *The Naïve and Sentimental Lover* . . . It's one of the le Carré titles.'

'That's good,' says Eve. 'I can see our man using that. Any other thoughts, anyone?'

'I don't like any of them,' says Billy.

'Any particular reason?' asks Claudia, closing her eyes and bowing her head.

'They just sound wrong,' says Billy.

'You don't think any of them are worth a try?' asks Eve. 'In any form?'

Billy shrugs. 'Not if we've only got three tries before we're locked out, no. We're not there yet.'

'Lance?'

'If Billy says we're not there yet, then we keep looking.'

'I'm sorry, everyone,' Eve mutters. 'You must be exhausted.'

Claudia and Zbig look at each other, but neither speaks.

'Those printouts,' says Niko. 'Shuffle them, then lay them all out again.'

Eve does so, and they stare at the A4 pages in silence. A minute passes, then another. Then, at the same moment, as if by telepathy, both Claudia and Niko place an index finger on the same sheet. It's a photograph of Penny Cradle with the children, Daniel and Bella, in a vast square in front of an ancient, pillared building. Penny is smiling a little fixedly, and the children are occupied with ice creams. In the bottom right-hand corner of the photograph someone, presumably Cradle, has written "Stars!".

'What?' says Eve.

'Not what. Why?' Claudia replies, and Niko smiles.

'I'm not with you,' says Eve.

'Why this photo?' says Niko. 'All the others are show-off shots, chosen to prove how important and successful this guy is. The high-profile acquaintances, the expensive long-haul holidays, the salmon fishing, and the rest of it. But this one's just . . . I don't know. The wife looks stressed, the kids look bored. Why does he call them stars? Why's the photo there?'

They all lean closer. 'Wait a minute,' says Zbig, his voice low. 'Wait a fucking minute . . .'

'Tell us,' says Eve.

'That square's in Rome, and the building behind them is the Pantheon. You can't see it, but there's a carved inscription on the front of it. *Marcus Agrippa, Lucii filius, consul tertium fecit*. Marcus Agrippa, son of Lucius, built this when consul for the third time.'

'So?'

'Wait till you see how it's actually written. Billy, can you Google "Pantheon inscription", and print us an image?'

Eve snatches the single sheet as it issues from the laser printer. Beneath the pediment of the building, the inscription is clearly legible:

M·AGRIPPA·L·F·COS·TERTIVM·FECIT

'Now that looks like a password,' says Claudia.

Eve nods. 'Billy?'

'I like it. Nice high entropy.'

'So let's try it.'

A flurry of keystrokes.

Access denied.

'Try just the letters without the spaces,' Eve suggests.

Billy does so, and this time Niko turns away, and Zbig swears in Polish.

Eve stares at the screen with exhausted eyes. She looks back at the A4 print, at the sunlit square and the family group, and something falls quietly and precisely into place. 'Billy, for the first attempt, you used upper-case letters and full stops, yes?'

He nods.

'But if you look at the inscription, those aren't full stops. They're symbols to mark the ends of the words, so that the inscription's legible.'

'Er . . . OK.'

'So try it again, but where you put full stops, put stars.'

'You're sure?'

'Do it,' says Eve.

A flurry of keystrokes, then silence.

'Christ on a bike,' breathes Billy. 'We're in.'

At the fashion house in the rue du Faubourg St Honoré, the anticipation is mounting. Like every haute couture show ever staged, this one is running late. No one is so gauche as to betray actual excitement, but there's an expectancy in the muted laughter, the flickering glances, and the delicate tapping of lacquered nails on iPhones. Villanelle closes her eyes for a moment, dismissing the crowd around her – the socialites overdressed for the press cameras, the fashion

212

professionals in shades of black – and inhales the heady perfume of wealth. The fragrance of the lilies, fuchsias and tuberoses banked on either side of the runway, and entwined with that, the smell of designer scent – Guerlain, Patou, Annick Goutal – on warm skin. And as a top note, the sharper odour of the sweat lending a faint sheen to the fore-heads of an audience that has been waiting here, on too-small gilt chairs, for more than forty minutes.

Absently, Villanelle reaches out and takes a rose-petal-flavoured Ladurée macaroon from the box on Anne-Laure's lap. As she closes her teeth on its crisp outer shell the lights dim, the shining peals of a Scarlatti cantata fill the space, and the first model swings out onto the runway, wearing a long, crocus-yellow silk coat. She's a vision, but Villanelle doesn't really register her.

What would happen, she wonders, if Lara Farmanyants were to announce that Oxana Vorontsova is alive. Would anyone believe her, or care? Who was Oxana Vorontsova, after all? Some crazy student who shot three gangsters in a Perm bar, and then supposedly killed herself in prison. Old news, long forgotten. Russia's a madhouse these days, and people are being murdered all the time. Why would Lara speak out? Who would she tell?

On the runway, immaculately tailored suits give way to embroidered crossover tops and tulle ballet skirts in dusty pink. Anne-Laure sighs appreciatively, and Villanelle helps herself to another macaroon, this one flavoured with Marie-Antoinette tea.

The point is not who she would tell, or who would care. The point is that if any element of the Villanelle legend threatens to unravel – if there's so much as a loose thread

213

– then she becomes a liability to the Twelve. And if that happens, she's dead. Which leads back to the necessity of killing Lara. But would she be able to get away with it? The Twelve have people everywhere. She could confide in Anton, but she doesn't fully trust him, and he might well decide that it is her, and not Lara, who has to be eliminated. Besides, she has to admit that she's stirred by Lara, with her unblinking sniper's gaze and hard, efficient body. She's excited by the poignancy of her need.

A Handel sarabande. Cocktail frocks in silvery grey, furled like unopened petals around the slender bodies of the models. Evening gowns in midnight blue, embroidered with galaxies of diamanté stars.

Shooting Konstantin was bad. The sudden nothingness behind his eyes. Did Anton fly her halfway across the world to kill him out of a perverse consideration? Or to deliver a brutal message to Villanelle about the reality of her situation?

What's most concerning is that the crisis in Odessa arose at all. It tells her that while the organisation that employs her is more than capable of solving its problems, it's also susceptible to error. Konstantin always gave her to believe that in working for the Twelve, he and she were part of something which was both invisible and invulnerable. This episode showed that for all its reach and power, the organisation could be hurt. Despite the warmth of the salon, Villanelle shivers.

The lights soften. The fashion show has progressed to the bedroom, to a dreamscape finale with the models swaying and weaving in delicate camisoles, sheer nightdresses, and shimmering organza gowns. The designer steps onto the runway, blows kisses at the audience, and is met by waves of applause. The models retreat, and waiters circulate with trays.

'So did you see any of that?' asks Anne-Laure, handing her a flute of pink Cristal champagne. 'You seemed miles away.'

'Sorry,' murmurs Villanelle, closing her eyes as the icy wine slides down her throat. 'I'm a bit zonked. I haven't slept much.'

'Don't tell me you want to go home, *chérie*. We've got the whole night ahead of us, starting with a party backstage. And there are two very handsome men over there, staring at us.'

Villanelle inhales the scented air. The champagne has set her body tingling. The exhaustion falls away, and with it, for now, the doubts and fears of the last twenty-four hours.

'OK,' she says. 'Let's have some fun.'

'So,' says Richard Edwards. 'Dennis Cradle. You're really sure about this? Because if you're wrong. If *we're* wrong—'

'We're not wrong' says Eve.

They're sitting in Edwards's thirty-year-old Mercedes in an underground car park in Soho. The grey-blue interior is worn but comfortable, the open windows admit a faint smell of exhaust.

'Run it past me again.'

Eve leans forward in her seat. 'Acting on information given to us by Jin Qiang, who almost certainly knows more than he's saying, we investigated a large payment made by persons unknown to a Gulf State account held by one Tony Kent. It turns out Kent is an associate of Dennis Cradle, and when we conducted a covert search of Cradle's property, we found a locked file concealed on his computer. When we broke the password and opened it, we discovered details of a numbered account in the British Virgin Islands owned by Cradle. We also discovered that a sum in excess of £12 million has recently been paid into this account by Tony Kent, from the account that he controls at the First National Bank of Fujairah. I'd say that was conclusive enough to act on.'

'So you want to bring Cradle in?'

'I propose that we have a quiet word with him. We don't mention these accounts and payments to anyone – Revenue, police, whoever. Instead, we leave everything in place. But we turn Cradle. We threaten him with exposure, shame, prosecution, whatever it takes, and we wring him dry. If he helps us, and agrees to let us run him against his paymasters, he gets to keep the money. If he doesn't, we throw him to the wolves.'

Edwards frowns, beating a soft percussion on the steering wheel with his fingers. 'If you're right about the people who are paying him . . .'

'I am right.'

He stares through the windscreen at the concrete walls, and the low ceiling with its sprinkler fittings. 'Eve, listen to me. There are enough dead people in this story. I don't want you and Dennis Cradle adding to their number.'

'I'll step carefully, I promise you that. But I want this woman, and I'm going to get her. She killed Viktor Kedrin on my watch, she killed Simon, and she's killed God knows how many other people besides.'

He nods, his expression grave.

'She's got to be stopped, Richard.'

Richard is silent for a moment, then sighs.

'You're right. She has. Do it.'

When Eve gets home, Niko is sitting at the kitchen table making calculations in a notebook. The table is littered with electrical components and cooking ingredients. He looks tired.

'So,' he asks her carefully. 'Did you find what you were looking for in that file?'

'Yes,' she says, kissing the top of his head, and subsiding into the chair next to his. 'We did. Thank you.'

'Excellent. Can you pass me that glass beaker?'

'What exactly are you doing?'

He attaches two wires to a multimeter with alligator clips, causing the needle to swing wildly. 'I'm making an enzyme-catalysed fuel cell. If I get this right, we should be able to charge our phones using icing sugar.'

'I'm sorry I've been so distant, Niko. Truly. I want to make it up to you'

'That sounds promising. Perhaps you could start by putting the kettle on?'

'Is this for the experiment?'

'No. I thought we might have a cup of tea.' He sits up and stretches out his arms. 'It's over, then, that project you were working on?'

Behind his back, she takes the Glock 19 pistol from her waistband holster and transfers it to her bag.

'No,' she says. 'It's just beginning.'

217

'It's just beginning.'

Continue reading with
NO TOMORROW
The next instalment in the Killing Eve series